Jingly Bells

A
California Belly Dance Romance
Holiday Novella

Book 4

Jingly Bells

A
California Belly Dance Romance
Holiday Novella

Book 4

DEANNA CAMERON

Fine Skylark Media
California

Fine Skylark Media
P.O. Box 1505
Lake Forest, California 92609-1505

Cover photography by Victoriaandreas via Dreamstime.com (dancer), feedough via Depositphoto.com (male model), and Makkuro via Depositphoto.com (ornament)

TITLES BY DEANNA CAMERON

PRAISE FOR *SHIMMY FOR ME*

"DeAnna Cameron delivers satisfying happily ever
afters that will leave you sighing."
        —Beth Yarnall author of *Wake Up Maggie*

"Cameron ensures that love triumphs in a delightful
and believable way."
                —Susan Squires, New York Times
                bestselling author of the Magic series

PRAISE FOR *THE BELLY DANCER*

"A beautifully written page-turner with characters that
leap off the page, *The Belly Dancer* transports readers
into an exotic and sensual world within a world, as
plucky but initially naive Dora Chambers fights
Chicago society's conventions and her husband's
indifference to discover, in the thrall of the Egyptian
Theatre, a passion beyond her wildest dreams."
                —Lynette Brasfield,
                author of *Nature Lessons: A Novel*

"The 1893 World's Fair was a marvel, and in her debut, Cameron uses this backdrop to demonstrate one woman's view of herself. Society is forever altered because of what she learns in the lush, sensual, and exotic world of belly dancers. With a strong and vibrant picture of the era and a feminist approach to history, Cameron makes statements about women's rights and society's constraints."

—RT Book Reviews (4 stars)

PRAISE FOR *DANCING AT THE CHANCE*

"Old New York comes to vibrant life in this dazzling tale of follies and illusions. *Dancing at The Chance* serves up a racy, exuberant feast for the senses, with a lively and intrepid heroine determined to succeed in a fading world threatened by fast-paced, fickle modernity."

—C.W. Gortner,
author of *The Confessions of Catherine de Medici*

"*Dancing at The Chance* took me back to Old New York, when vaudeville still enchanted audiences and Ziegfeld was king. In her second novel, DeAnna Cameron brings the world of 1900's theatre to vibrant life. Part circus, part Shakespeare, part Arabian nights, the Chance Theatre is a place I would love to visit again."

—Christy English, author of *To Be Queen*

DEDICATION

To all the readers who have reached out with praise for the California Belly Dance Romance series. Your encouragement means the world to me.

CHAPTER ONE

THE SULTAN'S TENT bar thumped and buzzed like a hormone-fueled frat party. A party where a girl could dance and drink and lose herself without even trying. A party that could make Tilly Bennett forget every reason she hated Christmas.

At least that was her plan.

She sat back on her barstool and soaked in the madness around her until her friend returned, emerging from the crowd with two martini glasses rimmed with crushed candy canes.

Abby sloshed one of the milky white cocktails when she handed it to Tilly. "This place isn't usually such a zoo. But I know the bartender. He'll take care of us."

Tilly stared at the creamy drink. A sick feeling clawed up the back of her throat. "I don't mind the zoo, but I'm not sure about *this*." She set the glass down and slid it back to Abby. "You can keep mine. I'm going to stay away from eggnog for a while."

She'd worked through dinner, helping Abby and her staff transform the Shimmy Shop's studio into a performance space for a couple dozen dance students and seating for their friends and family. The only thing she'd had that resembled food since breakfast was the eggnog chilling in the studio's mini fridge. Somehow, she'd managed to drink her way through a whole quart. The thought of one more drop made her stomach somersault.

"It's not eggnog." Abby sipped from hers. "It's melted ice cream with vodka and something minty. He called it a Christmas Wish. You should try it."

Tilly lifted the glass, but her attention skipped across the room to a guy in a thousand-dollar suit moving in on a career girl in a tweed mini dress. While Abby had been getting drinks, Tilly watched Shy Guy hover, trying to catch the girl's attention. She pegged him as a bashful, corporate type.

She'd been rooting for him to muster the courage to speak to the girl and now—finally!—he was striking up a conversation. The young woman swayed and giggled and twirled her California blond hair. Tilly silently urged him on. Someone should get a happy ending tonight.

He inched closer and pulled a sprig of mistletoe from his breast pocket.

That's when Tilly saw his wedding band. Its glint hit her like a brick of deja vu. Christmas was about to claim another casualty, and it didn't feel any better knowing this time it wouldn't be her.

She reached into her red leather clutch and found the hotel key card she'd picked up an hour before.

She rubbed it between her fingers like a worry stone, letting its smooth, solid surface soothe the pain that always returned this time of year.

"Do you really hate it?" Abby reached across the table to retrieve the martini glass. "I can ask him to make something else."

Tilly pulled her hand from her purse. "No, I'm sure it's fine." She turned her back on the couple and ignored the urge to march over and smack Shy Guy. She took a drink instead. It actually was good—sweet and minty with a coolness that gave way to a slow burn that melted her anger into a gooey pool of who-cares-anyway. She sipped again and nodded. "It's really good."

Abby lifted a thumbs-up sign to the long and lean hottie darting like a ping-pong ball behind the bar, trying to keep up with the thirsty eve of Christmas Eve crowd. "It's a winner, Marco," she hollered over the booming dance music. "Thank you."

Marco raised two fingers to his lips and tossed a quick kiss in their direction. "*Grazie, bella.*"

Tilly straightened and eyed Abby. Maybe Shy Guy wasn't the only one lining up mistletoe mischief. "Flirting with the Italian import? Better hope Derek doesn't find out."

Abby sputtered into her cocktail. "Marco? No way. He flirts with everybody. It's part of his charm."

Tilly wished she could reel back the accusation. "I don't know why I said that. Christmas makes me a little crazy."

"I think Christmas makes us all a little crazy." Abby winked and clinked her glass with Tilly's.

Tilly was working up a better explanation when the crowd parted and Melanie appeared.

"You didn't start the party without us, did you?" Melanie grabbed an empty stool from a nearby group and dragged it to the table. Behind her, three student dancers followed. Like Tilly and Abby, they were still in stage makeup and some combination of costume pieces and street wear.

"It took forever to get through the valet line." Melanie glanced back over her shoulder. "I thought Janaya was right behind me."

"Did I hear my name?" Janaya and her hot-pink dreadlocks swished into view, along with a few more student performers. When the greetings died down, Janaya threw her arms around Abby. "An after party was a fantastic idea. Thanks, boss."

Abby squeezed her. "It's the least I could do. You guys worked so hard to pull off the showcase. I'm beyond grateful, especially to Melanie and Tilly. I have no idea why either of you would work through your Christmas vacation, but we couldn't have done it without you."

Melanie dropped her head back and sighed. "Honestly? It feels good to be home. Being on tour is great, don't get me wrong, but I'm happy to be back in Orange County, even if it's just for a few days." She leaned over and jabbed at Tilly's shoulder. "I don't know how you do it. You've been touring for three years, practically non-stop. It's only been a few months for me, and I'm about to lose my mind. New York, London, Milan—so many great places, but they're becoming one, big, messy blur. How do you keep your sanity?"

"What sanity? That's the first thing to go in this business." She tipped her glass and drowned the uncomfortable knot in her throat.

An awkward silence settled on the table.

Melanie stared at her with wide, troubled eyes. "Please tell me you're joking."

"Of course I am." Her forced laugh uncorked a collective sigh of relief from the dancers around her, all except Melanie. There was something tender and raw in her expression that reminded Tilly of herself that first year, before the glamour of the traveling dancer's life wore off.

But those were her mistakes, not Melanie's.

Tilly locked on her friend's gaze. "Life on the road has its challenges, sure, but it has rewards, too. The fans. The perks. The parties. You can't let yourself forget that you're doing what thousands of girls dream of doing." It was the speech she told herself when the doubts set in.

She wished she still believed it.

"You're right. You guys are so lucky." Janaya flipped her dreadlocks over her shoulder and scooted her stool into the conversation. The students behind her murmured and nodded.

Abby leaned forward. "I'd say we were the lucky ones this week. We couldn't have pulled off this show without the extra help. So let's start this party off with a toast to Melanie and Tilly, our visiting Belly Dance Divas." She lifted her glass.

Melanie threw up her hands. "Wait! I need a drink. Who else?" She took a quick tally of raised hands. "Hold on, Ab. I'll be right back."

When she was gone, the attention returned to Tilly.

Abby rose and stood beside her. "I'm not kidding. The holiday show couldn't have happened without your help. With rehearsals, with classes, and with the costumes. I still can't believe you whipped up eight costumes in two days out of a single bolt of white stretch velvet."

The costumes. They'd been the highlight of the week. "I told you I love to sew. I'll take any opportunity I can to get behind a sewing machine. Teaching that beginning class was a first, but I enjoyed it, too. More than I thought I would."

Janaya slapped her hands on the table. "You've never taught beginners before? Ever? But you made it look so easy."

"I think you're just being kind, but thank you. I had a great time. I'm even a little sad it's over."

Abby snapped back from another conversation. "It doesn't have to be. You can come back any time. It's not usually this crazy, and I promise I can find something better than my couch for sleeping arrangements. I know I must owe your family a huge apology for monopolizing your time this week."

Tilly toyed with the stem of her glass and stared into the pool of white. "You don't owe anyone anything. Trust me." The truth of that tugged at something deep inside her, a loose thread she knew it was best to ignore.

Abby seemed too caught up in the moment to notice. "Think about the offer. We'd love to have you back."

"What offer?" Melanie returned to the table empty-handed. "Please tell me you aren't trying to lure Tilly away from the Divas the day before World Celebration?"

The annual multicultural show at the Orange County arts center was where the Divas debuted as a fledgling dance company four years before, and it was a sentimental favorite for the group's director.

"Garrett will kill me if she goes AWOL on my watch. He already hates me."

"Whoa, back up," Abby said. "I'm not asking anyone to leave the group. I'm just saying we'd love to have her back at the Shimmy Shop in the future. Maybe for a workshop between tours? Or anything Tilly wants to do."

"Thank goodness." Melanie dropped back into her seat with her usual, dramatic flair. "Then, go ahead. Continue. Tilly, what do you think?"

A half-dozen heads swiveled her direction. She didn't have an answer. It wasn't something she'd considered, but it was tempting. "I might be. Maybe a costume design workshop?"

Melanie scoffed. "Costumes? Seriously? You're a principal dancer in the Divas, and you want to teach people how to sew?"

"It's not just sewing. It's about imagining a look and bringing it to life. I'd almost forgotten how much I enjoyed that until I worked on the dresses for the Nefertiti routine this summer."

Melanie's dark eyes widened. "The turquoise and gold dresses with the lattice straps? You made those?"

"Designed them, too. And the *assuit* combo I wear in my second-act solo. I'd do more, if Garrett would let me."

Melanie snorted. "Why doesn't he? Those Nefertiti costumes are miles better than anything our costume department comes up with."

"Our seamstresses can barely keep up with repairs. He usually hires out the designing, but I know what you mean. I tried to talk to him about a few other ideas, but he's so busy."

"Busy. That's one way of putting it. I don't think he's spoken a word to me since he hired me."

Abby nudged Melanie's elbow. "Do you think that might have something to do with all the drama over your audition? It's probably better for you to stay off his radar for now anyway."

"It wasn't my fault." Melanie huffed and scratched at a groove in the tabletop. "But you're probably right."

Abby touched Tilly's arm lightly. "You can make costumes for us any time. For our showcases, for our boutique, whatever you want."

Behind Abby, Tilly spied Shy Guy shuffling toward the door, head down and shoulders hunched. She spied Miss Flirts-a-lot laughing and twirling her hair in a corner with someone new. She smirked. Maybe there wouldn't be any Christmas casualties tonight after all. Was it a sign? She laid her hand on her clutch and thought of the hotel room waiting for her at the end of the night. Maybe this year really would be different.

When she noticed Abby again, she was staring at her with her head cocked in a bemused sort of way.

"Why do you look like you just won the lottery?"

Tilly could feel her smirk stretching into a full-blown grin that tingled all the way down to her toes. "I don't know. I guess it's just been a great day. Good friends, a good show, good everything."

Marco approached the table, balancing a platter full of Christmas Wishes. Damn, he looked even better up close. Wide, tawny eyes, a sexy half-smile, and the kind of scruff that begged to be touched.

"Ladies, your drinks have arrived." There was that accent again, setting off a thousand tiny butterflies inside her. He put down the platter in the center of the table. "May I get you anything else?"

Maybe it was his accent or those full, pouty lips. Or maybe it was the Christmas Wish that made her lower her lashes and offer up her own sexy half-smile. "You know what they say. Flattery can get you everywhere."

If her flirtation surprised him, he didn't show it.

"I hope that's true, bella." He brought his palms together and raised his gaze to the heavens. "I pray—"

"Uh-oh." Abby stopped dispersing cocktails to the dancers behind her and fixed him with razor stare. "That sounds like you want something."

He clutched his heart and pretended to stagger. "I can hide nothing from you, bella. Yes, I have a question. Or perhaps you can call it a favor."

"A favor?" Tilly leaned forward. "Now this is getting interesting."

CHAPTER TWO

TILLY WAS ALWAYS a sucker for the tall, dark, and exotic ones, but there was something about Marco that put her in a mood to play. That quick smile and cocky tilt of his head. The way his black bangs flipped and fell over one eye. Those *cafe au lait* hands that jumped and gestured when he spoke. Yeah, she could watch him all night long.

"It is only a small favor." Marco pinched his forefinger and thumb together and flashed his adorable pearly whites. "A teensy favor."

Tilly sipped the last of her Christmas Wish and watched him bask in the attention of a table full of belly dancers.

"Our assistant manager quit yesterday, and a few things have fallen through the cracks. One of them was hiring the entertainment for tonight." He gestured and frowned in the direction of the bar's darkened stage. Then his expression brightened. His eyes twinkled. "But if you beautiful ladies were inclined to share your considerable talents—"

"You're asking us to perform?"

Abby's outburst put Marco on the defensive. His sheepish smile seemed to be all the answer she needed.

"No way." The shake of her head left no room for negotiation. "We just came from the studio's showcase, and Tilly and Melanie have a big show tomorrow. We couldn't possibly—"

"I don't mind." Tilly's words stopped Abby mid-sentence.

Marco turned and considered her. His lips twitched and he leaned closer. She could smell the sweet cinnamon scent of him, like those warm, gooey buns at the mall she could never resist. "Really? You would be willing?" He sounded as surprised as Abby and the others looked.

Her performer instincts kicked in. This wasn't Carnegie Hall or the Palladium, but she was in the spotlight. Marco's whiskey-colored gaze drank her in, and her whole body warmed. The way he licked his lips and caught his lower one in his teeth, she knew what he was thinking. She met guys like him on the road all the time. The smooth ones who could make a girl feel special with a look, at least until the next girl came along. And another girl always came along.

She wouldn't fall for that again. She'd keep the promise she'd made to herself: Keep it simple, and keep it solo. A perfect Christmas for one.

That didn't mean she couldn't have some fun with him, though.

She touched her ruby red lips with one ruby red fingernail and pretended not to notice him undressing her with his eyes. "But what would we get in return?"

With a good-natured grin, he threw up his arms and glanced down as if offering up himself. Every inch of him, from the broad shoulders straining the sleeves of his black button-down shirt to everything below. "You, bella, can have anything you want."

Men were so predictable.

"Anything?" She smirked but played along, letting her gaze drift from the top of his tousled bangs, down the length of him, over the hard lines of his scruffy jaw, his lean waist and hips, and the pointed tips of his black leather boots. He certainly wasn't the worst thing she'd seen that night.

Around her the Shimmy Shop women watched. Some snickered. Some held their breath. Some were probably wondering how far this would go.

Tilly trailed her fingernail across her lip, letting the uncertainty hang in the air. Despite herself, she was becoming as aroused as he seemed to be. "Let me think. What do I want?" She waited a beat, then two. "I know." She paused again. "How about, if we dance, we drink for free?"

His giddy smile vanished. His shoulders sank. "You want drinks?"

She heard more snickers from the dancers around her. She ignored them and nodded. "Just drinks."

Was his disappointment sincere or was he playing the game, too? It didn't matter. She turned to the rest of her group. "What do you think, ladies? Are you willing to dance for our drinks?"

The question was met with a hearty round of agreement.

She swiveled back to Marco. "I think that'll do it." She pushed her empty glass his direction. "These Wishes seem to be doing the trick. How about we start with another round of these?"

He reached across the table to take her glass. She stopped him before he could pull the glass away, and wrapped her fingers around his own.

His head shot up.

"If you wouldn't mind, could you throw an extra splash of holiday spirit in mine? I'm feeling a little naughty."

He stood there, frozen and staring at her. He shook it off. "Of course. Extra spirits. Anything else?"

She slid her hand away and settled back in her chair, pleased with herself. "No. Just that."

He opened his mouth and closed it twice. Finally, he found his voice. "Another round of Christmas Wishes for the dancers then." He flashed his perfect, pearly white smile at her. "If you think of anything else, you'll let me know. Right, bella?"

CHAPTER THREE

MARCO RAN HIS stainless steel shakers under hot water, swished them with soap, and tried to keep his mind on his job—and off the woman who had just played him for a fool.

It wasn't working.

When Abby slid into a space between a guy in a suit putting the moves on a woman half his age and a crew of computer types from the local office park, he welcomed the distraction.

"So, the assistant manager position opened up. That's interesting." She grabbed a maraschino cherry from his stash and popped it into her mouth.

Should I get you an application?"

"Not me. I was thinking for you."

He knew what she was thinking. Ever since he'd made the mistake of telling her about his hospitality business management degree, she'd been pressing him to get a better job. He told her the same thing he always told her. "It's not a good time."

"When will it be a good time?"

When life wasn't so complicated. When he didn't have more important things to worry about. "I'll do it when I'm ready."

She sighed. At least she knew when to let the subject drop.

"I'm sorry about the drinks," she said. "You can put them on my tab. I don't want you to get in trouble."

"The drinks are no problem." He lifted the shakers from the sink and wiped them with the towel off his shoulder. "But your friend—"

The pink-haired dancer pushed by Casanova and his prey and pressed herself against the counter beside Abby. "I can't find the cord to plug my phone into the sound system. Could you help me?" She leaned in, giving him a clear shot of her ample cleavage.

He pretended not to notice and focused on filling the shakers with ice. "It's the yellow one on top of the unit." He pointed the ice scoop in the general direction and told her which switches activated the system.

She sucked her fuchsia lips into a pout and leaned until the black lace of her top strained to keep her assets contained. "But could you come over and show me?"

Behind her a few of the girls at the table had their heads together, giggling. One peeked in his direction.

But it wasn't the one with the blond curls. She was turned away from the others, watching a dancer who had already taken the stage.

"It's easy, bella." He plunged the scoop into the ice bin. "You'll figure it out."

She straightened and tugged at her top's midriff hem. "Fine. Your loss." She stomped back to her table.

He caught Abby sucking in a grin.

"What?" Should he be annoyed? Embarrassed?

"Nothing." She stole another cherry. "I'm just surprised. Isn't she your type?"

He filled a shaker. "I have no type."

"Really? I used to work here, remember? Back then your type was 'has a pulse.' Tell me I'm wrong."

He stabbed the scoop deep into the ice to break apart the frozen blocks that formed below the surface. He stabbed to cool the anger churning in his gut. He stabbed until his fingers turned to prickly stone. "Maybe then. Not now." He stabbed again.

She reached over the bar and stopped his hand. "I'm sorry. I shouldn't have said that. I was just teasing."

He forced himself to stop, to breathe, to meet her gaze instead of slinking off. "Of course. It's been a long day."

She didn't look convinced. "What were you going to ask me? Something about one of my friends."

He already regretted saying anything. Better to forget it. Forget her. "Don't you need another drink?" He raised a shaker and wiggled it. Where was a rush on drinks when he needed one? Now that the crowd had some entertainment, they had drifted from the bar to the stage for a better view.

"You aren't getting off that easily." Abby looked over her shoulder at the table of dancers. "You were talking about Tilly, weren't you?"

He followed her gaze. Yeah, that was the one. He grabbed the carafe of melted vanilla ice cream, the vodka, and the liqueurs and mulled the name. Tilly. It had a ring to it. Pleasant, but feisty, too. "Is she new?"

Triumph brightened Abby's face. "I knew it. She is new, but she's just visiting."

Probably just as well. He filled a shaker, capped it, and shook.

The phone in his pocket buzzed. He put down the shaker, pulled out his phone, and held up a finger to Abby. He turned away and read the name on the screen. Maria. He'd told her not to call him at work unless it was an emergency, and his gut told him this wasn't an emergency. He let the call go to voice mail and he turned back to Abby, but he couldn't focus. He started on the next shaker but over-poured the vodka. He dumped it down the drain and started again.

"So, about Tilly," Abby said when he went back to shaking. "She's a Belly Dance Diva, and their tour is taking a break for the holiday. It starts up again in a few days. Not sure when exactly, but I could ask her. I mean, if you want me to."

"No, forget it." He set down the second shaker and readied the third.

"Are you sure?"

Why had he said anything? There was nothing worse than a woman who sensed romantic interest, especially when it involved a friend.

He sighed and returned her penetrating glare. "I'm sure." He reached up and grabbed fresh martini glasses hanging by their stems above the counter and made a row of them. Everything would be fine if he just stuck to work.

"All right. Be that way." Abby pulled away, defeated. She'd taken a couple steps when she turned back. "I almost forgot why I came up here in the first place. There's something I wanted to ask you."

"The drinks are almost ready. Two minutes." He dipped the rim of a glass in a syrup solution and then a platter of crushed candy canes. *Focus on work. Focus on the job. Forget the phone call.*

"Not the drinks." She stared at him, long and hard. "Are you all right?"

Was it so obvious?

He looked up and unleashed his secret weapon, his life-is-good-and-I'm-even-better smile. The toothy, confident grin that could always be counted on to get a phone number or a second chance. "I'm fantastic, bella." He threw his hands out wide. "And how are you?"

It worked. Her eyes twinkled and her lips twitched into a smile of her own. "I'm good."

"Just good? Not great? Not fantastic?"

"Okay, I'm fantastic."

He punched the air. "Yes! That's what I like to hear."

"Okay, we're both fantastic." Her laughter trickled away. "But here's the thing. I bought flowers—an obscene number of flowers—to decorate the studio for tonight's showcase, and it occurs to me they're going to go to waste because we'll be closed until

18

after New Year's. I'd like to find them a new home and I was wondering..." She glanced around the bar. "Do you think your boss would like to have them for the restaurant?"

"She'd love it." His enthusiasm earned him another frown, but he didn't care. He'd been braced for more uncomfortable questions, and all she wanted was a home for orphan flowers. "How many flowers exactly?"

"Six, maybe seven bouquets. Big bouquets. Red roses, white lilies, lots of green stuff."

He pictured the flowers his mother grew on their balcony back in Florence. She'd cut and arrange them into bouquets to fill the house, even during the holidays. Every year she obsessed about her centerpiece for the Christmas feast like other mothers obsessed about their tomato gravy, braised meat, and sweet panettone.

"You can bring them, definitely. But, maybe, if you don't mind, I have another suggestion."

CHAPTER FOUR

BY ELEVEN-THIRTY, the Shimmy Shop women were the last party at the Sultan's Tent bar. By midnight, even the dancers were drifting toward the door.

"You aren't leaving already, are you?" Tilly eyed Abby fondling her keys as she watched Janaya on the stage. "I thought we could pull everybody together for a circle dance or some tribal-style improv."

Abby stifled a yawn. "I'd love to, but I'm beyond exhausted. Aren't you?"

"No way. The night is young. Parties don't end at midnight. The good ones are just getting started."

Abby grabbed her phone. "It's midnight already?" She tapped her screen, looking for confirmation. Getting it, she dropped her head back and sighed. "No wonder I'm beat."

"Beat? C'mon, you have another dance in you. I know you do."

Abby rubbed her forehead and yawned. "You spent all day helping me set up the showcase, then you danced at the showcase, then we came here and danced again. Why do you look like you could go till dawn? How's that even possible?"

She lifted her empty Christmas Wish and wiggled it. "Sugar high?"

It was meant to be a joke, but it wasn't far off. She'd had at least five of the sweet drinks. If she hadn't stuffed herself with hummus and pita bread, and just about everything else on the appetizer menu, she probably wouldn't be able to stand, let alone dance.

She could see Abby wasn't buying it. She tried again. "I mean, why sleep when you're having fun with friends, right?"

That was closer to the truth, but the real truth was she wouldn't be thinking about sleep for a long time. Not when every twinkle from the holiday lights strung along the walls and every flash of tinsel and shiny glass balls on the fake Douglas fir beside the stage reminded her of things she didn't want to remember. Things she could always stuff into a corner like old clothes, except this time of year.

She stared hard at Janaya undulating onstage to a slow, thumping rhythm and waited for the iceberg in her throat to melt.

Abby's usually porcelain smooth forehead creased with concern. "Are you sure that's it?"

"Absolutely." She slipped back into her life-of-the-party-girl smile. "Never better."

"Are you still planning to crash at your aunt's place tonight?"

Her aunt? Oh, her aunt. It was the lie she'd told Abby at breakfast when she'd asked about her Christmas plans. She hadn't intended to deceive her, but she knew what happened when she told people the truth. They never understood that Christmas was just another day to her. Nothing special and certainly nothing to celebrate. They never believed she could be that ambivalent, so inevitably they tried to include her in their own plans, which meant invitations to family gatherings where she'd be an awkward outsider forced into uncomfortable conversations with strangers.

At eight in the morning, before her first cup of coffee, it was more than she could face, so a fictitious aunt came to her rescue. It had been an innocent, little lie. At first. But as the caffeine hit her bloodstream, the story grew, and so did the lie. By her third cup, she'd invented a full Christmas weekend at a cozy beach bungalow where there would be nieces and nephews, cousins and grandparents. A bleeping menagerie of Christmas cheer.

Remorse had hit even before the java jitters wore off. She wanted to take her tall tales back, but it was too late. Better to just steamroll through the holiday and the lie, and then everything would go back to normal. That morning, on the drive between Abby's apartment and the studio, with her suitcases in the back, she'd formulated her plan.

Who needed a family to get quality time at the beach? She could make her own holiday getaway. When she passed the towering Newport Beach Bay Club and Resort on her way to the restaurant, she did a U-turn and pulled into the palm tree-lined driveway. At the glass and brass revolving door, she hesitated, but only for a second. A cordial staffer behind the marble-cut counter beckoned her forward. From there, it was a credit card swipe, a signature, and she was the new, if temporary resident of room three-fifty-two—a room that promised a panoramic oceanfront view, complimentary continental breakfast, and not a single reminder that it was Christmas.

All hers, and all a plastic key card away.

"Yeah, she gave me the key." The key card was right there in her purse, so technically, it wasn't a lie.

"Wouldn't it be easier to stay at my place tonight? You'll be closer to the theater, and it's really no problem."

She shook her head. "I promised." Again, technically not a lie.

Abby leaned back in her chair and her eyelids fluttered. She closed them. "Okay. I don't know about you, but I'm going to sleep as late as possible tomorrow. I just have to get to the studio at some point to clean up, then get to Derek's family thing. Did I tell you? We're going to his dad's house for a family dinner."

"Spending the holidays with the boyfriend's family, huh? That sounds cozy."

Abby's eyes popped open and she smirked. "I doubt it. He's already warned me that *family dinner* means at least sixty people, a catered meal with a wait staff, and formal attire. Formal!"

"Oh."

"I'd take your beach bungalow holiday any day. Maybe I should tag along with you. Do you think your aunt would mind?"

Tilly coughed and bit her lip. After everything Abby had done for her, she couldn't say no. But she absolutely couldn't say yes. She stole a glance back at the hottie bartender refilling liquor bottles behind the counter and wondered if it was too late to order another round of holiday spirit. Instead, she shot up from her chair and nearly toppled the table. "I'll be back in a minute. That last drink went right through me."

She took two steps toward the ladies' room, then pivoted back. "If you leave before I get back, thanks again for everything." She bent down and gave Abby a hurried hug.

"What? Yeah. Of course. It was my pleasure." Abby's surprised expression dipped into a frown. Then she glanced at Marco. A mischievous grin crept across her face. "I get it. *Merry* Christmas."

CHAPTER FIVE

MARCO SLIPPED THE towel off his shoulder and wiped up the circles of condensation on the bar's polished wood counter. Should he knock on the ladies' room door to see if Abby's friend was all right? He glanced again at the digital clock beneath the counter. One-twelve. She'd been in there a long time.

He tossed the towel over his shoulder and went around the room, clearing the last of the tables and flipping on the house lights.

He should have asked Abby to check in there before she left. That would've been the smart thing to do. Now there was no one to do it but him. Not that it would be the first time he'd have to help a drunk customer who'd fallen asleep in there, or worse. It was one of the hazards of the job. But why her? She hadn't seemed drunk. More than any of the Shimmy Shop women, she'd seemed the soberest, despite the cocktails she'd put away.

Free cocktails.

He wiped down another table and sighed. She'd earned every one of them, too. He'd had a hell of a time keeping orders straight when she was on the stage. When she'd leaned back and dropped to her knees in what somebody at the bar had called a Turkish drop, he'd nearly dumped a strawberry margarita on a woman. He probably should have felt bad about that, but who orders a strawberry margarita at Christmas? He shook his head. Only in Southern California. You'd never see that back home.

So, maybe there was another reason she was taking her time...

He kept working and hummed one of the slower, sexier tunes she'd danced to earlier.

When she finally emerged ten minutes later, he was back behind the counter. She breezed by on her way to her table and didn't seem at all surprised to find they were the last people left in the place.

"I'm glad to see you're all right, bella." He watched her as he punched his code into the cash register to run the night's tally.

"I'm fine, thank you."

The words were quick and crisp. No slurs. Good sign. But also not open to further conversation. Bad sign. She was clearly not interested.

Probably for the best.

He watched her grab her purse off the table. She searched for something else. "I don't see the check. How much do I owe you?"

Another time he'd have a dozen suggestive answers to that question, but not tonight. It was too late. He was tired. She wasn't interested. "On the house. No charge."

"The drinks, yeah, but all the food? I'm happy to pay what I owe."

He shook his head. "On the house."

Across the room he could see her grimace and her eyes turned glassy. Were those tears? She turned away before he could be sure.

"Thank you." She sniffed, tucked her purse beneath her arm, and made her way to the door in long, determined strides.

"Wait." Why had he said that?

She stopped and glared at him. He wanted to disappear.

"What?" She sniffed, locked her arms over her chest, and dipped her head so he couldn't see past her blond curls.

He should ask. *Just ask.* What did he have to lose?

But the question died in his throat.

He flipped his towel over his shoulder. "I just wanted to say, I hope you have a happy holiday."

She chuckled softly in a joyless sort of way. "Right. Happy holidays." The door latched with a heavy thud behind her.

CHAPTER SIX

TILLY STOOD BENEATH the misty half moon and kicked herself for not remembering where she parked. She'd spent the past forty-five minutes in the lavatory hiding from Abby. At least that's how it started. Sitting on a velvet cushion in front of the vanity mirror, waiting for the guilt and self-loathing to subside. Then came the tears. The snot. The overflowing bin of soggy, used tissues.

One good look at herself in the mirror, with the runny mascara, bloodshot eyes, and smeared lipstick snapped her out of it. What did she have to snivel about? She had an incredible hotel room waiting for her. Sure, it cost more than she made in a month, but she'd be sleeping between sheets with a thread count in the thousands. She could have chocolate and champagne delivered to her door. When the sun came up, she'd have the Pacific Ocean at her feet. Maybe she'd even take an early morning dip.

Life wasn't bad. In fact, it was very good.

Being alone didn't change that. Once she cocooned herself in the hotel room, she'd feel better. She just had to get there. She marched out of the restaurant door and into the frigid night air rolling in off the coast. Goosebumps crawled up her arms and she pulled her black Spanish shawl from her hips to her shoulders. It wasn't much protection from the cold, but it was something.

She stared into the parking lot that had been packed with vehicles when she arrived. Now it was dark and lonely, and the damp cold threatened rain.

Where was that stupid car?

She remembered doing a lap, then two. She was on the fourth when a spot finally opened up.

Where had that been?

There weren't many options. The lot had five rows, with some additional parking along the back concrete wall. She could see most of it, thanks to the hazy light cast from two light poles, so that meant her little hatchback was hiding behind one of the larger, abandoned vehicles scattered across the lot.

She walked along the closest aisle, expecting to see her tiny black car dwarfed behind one SUV or another. When she reached the concrete wall that separated the lot from its neighbor, she frowned.

It wasn't possible. Not now. Not at Christmas for Pete's sake.

She hurried down the next aisle. And the next.

A shimmer of glass pebbles scattered near one of the light poles caught her attention. She tugged the shawl more tightly around herself and walked toward it.

It wasn't just a few shards, but a wide swath of them. Some as large as a dime, most smaller than a pinhead. Hundreds, thousands of tiny flecks of light. She recognized the scatter pattern of a smashed-out car window.

In the shaft of ghostly light, she noticed something else: a sticker slapped on the light pole's concrete base from one of her favorite fish taco shops.

She closed her eyes.

It wasn't. It couldn't.

The black silk shawl fell from her shoulders, and what remained in her stomach of that last cocktail lurched up her throat. It took everything she had not to fall to her knees and let go of the sobs gripping her chest.

A sound stopped her. A scraping like footsteps in the darkness behind her. She froze.

"Don't come any closer." Her voice trembled. "I'll scream. My friends are inside. You'll—"

"It's me, bella."

She whipped around to find Marco standing in the shadows, the tips of his black hair glowing in the faint moonlight.

She'd never been so happy to see another human being.

He hurried toward her and scooped up the shawl from the ground. He shook off the dust and draped it back over her shoulders. His touch was soft and warm.

"Are you okay?" Concern carved canyons into his chiseled features.

She hugged her shoulders and stared into the empty parking space beneath the light pole. "It's gone." The words nearly choked her.

"What? Your car? It's not possible. It must be here. Perhaps you parked somewhere else. Come, we'll look together. What kind of car is it?"

"A black Celica."

He frowned.

She knew that look. "Yeah, I know. Who would steal a fifteen-year-old Toyota, right?"

"Don't jump to conclusions. We'll find it." He scanned the darkened lot, but she didn't need to look. She knew. She remembered the sticker. She'd noticed it when she opened her car door. She'd made the mental note to stop in before she left town.

As this new certainty soaked in, the panic waned. Something hard and cold took its place.

"It was stolen." She swallowed the last of the fear, the last of the hope that she was wrong. "It's gone. All of it. Everything."

Saying the words made it real. The pain, the regret, the disbelief vanished. She was empty.

He pulled his phone from his pocket.

She stopped his arm. "What are you doing?"

"Calling the police."

"No. Please."

His expression twisted. "You have to report it."

What difference would a report make? Her life was gone.

"Not tonight."

"They can't help if you don't call."

She shook her head. She was never going to spend another Christmas anywhere near a police station, but she wasn't about to explain that to a guy she barely knew, even if he smelled like the best damn snickerdoodle you could imagine.

"I'm tired. I just want to crawl into bed and deal with it later."

She didn't have to give up. She had the key card.

He shook his head. "You have to let the police come. The thieves might have left something behind that can help.

She stared into the constellation of glass shards. Interspersed among them were a few pebbles, a dusty penny, something that looked like it might have been a french fry.

All those hours wasted in a police station four years ago came screaming back to haunt her. Filling out all those police forms. Talking to all those police officers. Pretending she didn't hear all their whispers. *"Such a shame. Such a tragedy. And at Christmas, can you imagine?"*

She pushed the memories away. Stuffed them back into the black hole where they lived.

"There's nothing here," she said. "There's no point."

She pulled out her own phone.

"Are you calling?"

"I'm getting a ride." She tapped her phone screen and swiped until she found her ride share app.

He took her hand and held it, entwined his warm, strong fingers between her cold ones.

She wanted to pull away, but she couldn't move. She stared at their hands. At her skin pressed against his.

When she didn't resist, he pulled her closer. His soft, velvety brown gaze bore down on her. "Don't. I know you're upset, but you should stay and make the report. Don't give up hope."

Standing so close, she couldn't think of anything but the wisps of his warm breath, the dusky tint of his lips, the power in his grip. She couldn't have pulled away if she tried, but she didn't want to try.

CHAPTER SEVEN

MARCO SPREAD PLASTIC wrap over two chicken breasts and pounded out his frustration until they were both even, quarter-inch-thick filets. He was dredging them through egg and flour when Tilly walked through the kitchen's swinging doors looking calmer than she had when he'd found her in the parking lot nearly an hour before.

"Any luck?" He finished the chicken and soaped his hands under the faucet in water as hot as he could stand.

"The good news is I got through to a real person at the insurance company." She slid onto a stool alongside the stainless steel counter that ran down the center of the kitchen, separating the cooking line from the wait station. "The bad news is they won't authorize a car rental or anything until I get a police report."

He dried his hands and fired up one of the industrial-sized burners. "A police report? How interesting."

It was a cheap shot, but he couldn't help it. She should have listened to him.

"Smug is not your color. But, yeah, I called the police. Or tried to."

"What happened?" He grabbed a fry pan from a lower shelf and set it on the flame.

"I called 9-1-1 but apparently having your car stolen isn't an emergency unless you're watching it happen." She planted her elbows on the table and dropped her chin on her knuckles. "The dispatcher, who was at least nice about brushing me off, gave me the non-emergency number to call, which I did. I sat on hold for twenty minutes before they told me I'd have to wait at least an hour for an officer to come by."

"So then, the news was not all bad."

Her lips twisted. "How do you figure?"

He chuckled and grabbed the plastic squirt bottle beside the stove. "You get to spend more time with me." He swirled a stream of oil into the pan and waited for her comeback.

There wasn't one.

When he glanced over his shoulder, she had that million-mile stare again. Then her lips quivered.

"Hey, hey, hey." He wiped his hands on a dishtowel and leaned over the table. "Everything will be all right. You can replace a car. You can replace your stuff. It's all just stuff. The important thing is you are okay."

The quivering stopped. She swallowed hard and pulled her shoulders back. "You're right. It's just stuff." She rubbed her forehead. "I'm not usually like this."

He could see her pain. It was lurking in the watery blue gaze that wouldn't meet his and the worry lines creasing her brow.

In an instant, the desire to make her laugh became something else. Something powerful and raw that pierced through his guilt. He rounded the table that separated them and slowly, deliberately, reached for her chin. When she didn't pull away, he lifted it and waited for her hesitant gaze to meet his. "You have nothing to be sorry about. I am the one who is sorry. You should have been safe here."

It was the thought that had been hammering at him from the moment he found her standing in the darkness. The one he'd been trying to ignore. He'd known it was late. He'd known she was alone. He should have done the right thing and walked her out, not run after her when it could have been too late.

What if it *had* been too late?

He snapped away and stalked back to the stove. He grabbed the fry pan with a towel and shook it violently over the burner, forcing the chicken to separate from the steel but doing nothing to free him from those regrets.

"This isn't your fault."

The fear in her voice brought him back to the moment, and he regretted the outburst. His temper was too quick these days. "I'm sorry." A hearty portion of shame heaped onto his remorse. "But it shouldn't have happened. Our lot should be safe. What if you'd been hurt?"

She softened, rose from the stool, and joined him at the stove. "But I wasn't hurt, no one was, and it is only stuff. Nothing important."

He answered by tossing a second chicken breast into the pan, making it sing with sizzling, sputtering oil.

As he worked, she inched closer until she was beside him. From his peripheral vision, he watched her smooth, porcelain arms, her glossy red fingernails. He watched the golden bangles that encircled her wrist and the tan freckles scattered around her elbow. The red halter's skinny straps wrapped around her neck, leaving her shoulders enticingly bare. What would it be like to undo those straps? To touch that pale, white skin?

When his glance reached her eyes, she was staring at the chicken crackling in the pan.

She must have felt his attention because she turned. "What?" Her fingers shot up to her reddening cheek and her glance darted away. "I look atrocious, don't I?" She hurried back to the other side of the room. "I'm sure all that blubbering did a number on my face."

"No. You look fine."

Fine? That was the best he could do? But it was too late. She was back at the stool with the hard slab of steel between them, staring into a compact mirror she'd pulled from her purse. She patted her nose with powder. He tried a different approach.

"I'm making chicken parm. There's enough for two, if you're hungry."

She laughed, a musical laugh like a dozen tiny bells. "So, you rescue damsels in distress and you cook, too? Your girlfriend's a lucky girl."

He focused on the pan, not trusting himself to look anywhere else, especially not at her. He stared at the chicken's edges turning a crispy golden brown, just as Ma had taught him. "I don't have a girlfriend. But thank you for asking."

His heart thundered in his chest, rattling his thoughts and unsettling his nerve. Was that too presumptuous? Had he proved himself a fool again? It was his turn to feel the burn shoot up his neck.

"Actually, I am hungry." She snapped her compact closed and tucked it away. If he'd offended her, she wasn't showing it. "I hope it's all right for me to be back here. I don't want to get you in trouble."

"It's fine." The words were short and curt, and he regretted them instantly. What was wrong with him? "I mean, I always cook after my shift. It's part of our deal." He shook the pan and jerked it, sending the breasts into a mid-air somersault.

"Wow, fancy. You could be a chef."

He pictured the men and women who worked long hours in this kitchen, most of them for paychecks that barely covered the rent. He shook his head. "I don't want to be a chef. I will run my own restaurant someday, not just the kitchen."

Her smile vanished. "I didn't mean to offend you. It was a compliment. It's just obvious you can cook. I can't. Like, at all."

He wanted to sink into a crack in the floor. He should apologize, but he didn't trust himself to say another word. Everything that came out of his mouth made things worse. He stared into the pan and bit his tongue.

She didn't speak, either. Not for a while. When he couldn't stand the silence, he stole a glance back at her. She looked so passive, so quiet and introspective. He couldn't break that calm. Instead, he grabbed the bowl of marinara sauce he'd prepared and ladled it carefully around the chicken, drenching it and his overwhelming urge to break the silence.

"My mom could cook," she said when the sauce bubbled and he'd nearly given up hope she'd ever say anything again. "She was a really good cook. She tried to teach me sometimes, but I was never interested. I was always too busy or had something else to do."

When her voice trailed off, he glanced back, silently urging her to continue but still not trusting his own voice. She had that faraway look again, but this time there was a sadness, too. It felt all too familiar.

"You said *was*—is she gone?" He couldn't resist. He had to know. Even if it was the wrong thing to say, even if she hated him for saying it. He had to know.

Her answer was a single, solemn nod. She touched the corner of her eye.

His chest contracted around the hollow space inside him, the empty place he filled with endless, worthless distractions. He gripped the pan's handle until his knuckles ached and the stone in his throat disappeared. When he could manage it, he whispered four words. "I'm so sorry, bella."

CHAPTER EIGHT

BELLA. TILLY HAD to admit, that silly word was growing on her. It had seemed like just another throw-away flirtation, but now it was something else. It was sweet and friendly. It was sincere. And right now it was as soft and warm as a tender embrace.

"It wasn't recent." She tensed despite herself. "There was a car accident a few years ago, before the Divas." She closed her eyes and saw her mother's face rimmed by wild blond curls like her own and the same silvery blue eyes. "She's the reason I became a Diva. I was in college, majoring in fashion design and hoping to land a job in a costume department or something backstage. I took belly dance classes for fun. When the Divas started up, she urged me to try out."

"Smart lady. She must have seen your potential."

"I guess. She always wanted to be a professional dancer. It had been her biggest regret, she said, letting her fear of failure stop her from pursuing that dream. She told me I had the talent, and I shouldn't let fear hold me back, too. She made me promise."

Her voice caught, and the memory flooded back. The telephone call. The nurse explaining about the accident. The long hours in her mother's hospital room and that conversation when her mother had finally woken up after surgery. She'd been so lucid, so aware of everything. They'd talked about the audition and so many things. Her mother had even reminded her to take the turkey out of the freezer so it would thaw in time for Christmas dinner.

The next day the aneurysm ended everything.

Marco set down the pan and reached across the table for her hands. His grip was strong and protective.

She blinked back the tears she refused to spill and looked up to see his eyes shimmering with their own emotion. The edges of his lips twitched.

"It's a terrible thing to lose your mother." The words snagged on the jagged edges of his voice. "I know."

He winced, unable to continue, and then she knew.

"You lost your mother, too?" She stared at his fingers. The tiny black hairs on the back of his hand. The white crescent moons of his neatly trimmed nails.

His lips parted to speak, then gave up and clamped closed again.

He didn't need to say it. In that moment she knew he understood all the pain and loneliness that comes from losing the person who has been with you from the beginning. Your cheerleader and your guardian. Your teacher and your friend.

The person who was there when anyone else you've ever depended on walked out and whose absence leaves a chasm in your life that nothing can fill.

She held his hands, and they stayed there, connected in the silence. For a long moment, she stared at the soft ridges of his knuckles and wondered how those fingertips would feel against her skin.

Her pulse quickened. Her breath shook.

When he lifted a finger to brush along her cheek, she jerked back.

"I'm sorry," he said. "I didn't mean to—"

"No." She tried to smile through her embarrassment. "It's all right. I mean, this is stupid, right? You don't even know me, and I don't know you. This is nuts."

She turned away to get some air, or a drink, or anything to put some distance between them.

He touched her hand again and pulled her back.

"Maybe it is nuts." He locked on her gaze and held it like he'd never let go. "Maybe I don't know you. But I'd like to."

CHAPTER NINE

MARCO LIFTED TILLY'S hand to his lips and gently kissed each finger, sending shivers through her that had nothing to do with the temperature in the room and everything to do with the smoldering heat in his eyes.

This was nuts. It was crazy.

But maybe she didn't care. Life was crazy. And since when did her life make sense anyway?

She'd lost everything that made sense four years ago, and she'd lost it again tonight.

What was left?

Just this. The way he touched her. The way he watched her. The way he made her feel so awake, so alive.

She thought of her empty hotel room and that perfect Christmas for one. Maybe that wasn't what she wanted at all. Every nerve, every muscle, every breath told her this is what she wanted. Him. And her. A cozy Christmas for two.

She was caught up in the possibility when he released her and returned to the stove. He lifted the lid he'd put over the simmering chicken.

"Are you ready to eat?" He dipped a teaspoon into the tomato sauce to test the sauce.

"Eat?" Who could eat? But the savory aroma of the chicken triggered a rumbling in her stomach she couldn't ignore. "Yeah, I guess I could eat."

He grabbed two plates from a rack. On each, he twirled a mound of spaghetti noodles that had been draining in the sink, then on top he placed the chicken, a ladle of steaming marinara, and a thick strip of white cheese.

"Come with me." He grabbed the plates and led her back to the bar. "What can I get you to drink?"

She stared at the wall of liquor bottles behind the counter and the memory of all those Christmas Wishes did somersaults in her belly. "Just water."

He set the plates on the counter. "You can have anything. It's still on the house."

She knew she was supposed to be looking at the bottles, but she couldn't take her eyes off the snug fit of his black jeans. "Tempting. But an officer will be here any minute. It would probably be better if I didn't slur my way through the report."

He sighed. "Good point. How about something without all the holiday spirit then?"

"Did you have something in mind?"

That mischievous twinkle returned to his eye. "I do."

He grabbed a shaker, dropped in three fresh cherries, and muddled them. He scooped in ice, added a dash of pomegranate juice and some orange juice, then shook. Through the strainer he poured the mixture into a tall glass until it was half-filled, then filled the rest with seltzer water and dropped another cherry on top. He pushed it her direction. "My virgin holiday special."

"Looks good." She picked it up and sipped. "Tastes even better. What do you call it?"

He crossed his arms. "I don't know. I just invented it. Maybe you should name it."

"I don't think so."

"Why not?"

"I've never done that before."

"There's nothing to it. You just think of a name. What are you afraid of?"

She straightened. "I'm not afraid."

He answered with a shrug.

"Fine." She sipped again and wiped her lips. "Okay. It's sweet. It's red. It's the holidays." She tapped her finger on the bar and thought of the possibilities. "How about Santa's Kiss?"

"Nope. Taken. Try again."

She grumbled. "Okay. How about Rudolph's Nose?"

"Taken."

"Really?" She pushed out her lower lip in an exaggerated pout. "I give up."

He cocked his head to the side. "Already? You don't strike me as the kind of woman who gives up so easily."

There was that irritating, but adorable half-smile again.

She shot him back a half-smile of her own. "If I didn't know better, I'd say you're flirting with me."

He slid onto the stool beside her. "Maybe that's exactly what I'm doing."

Was it getting warmer in here? She wrapped both hands around the cold, wet glass, seeking relief or a distraction. Maybe both.

"Unless you have a boyfriend." He pulled back. "If you do, then I'm definitely not flirting. Especially if he's big and mean and has a name like Gunter."

"What? You'd give up so easily?" She tried not to giggle, but she couldn't help it. "But no. No boyfriend. Not at the moment anyway."

"Gunter's loss." He slid back onto the seat again. Closer this time.

She nudged his elbow with her own. "Abby was right. You are a charmer."

He grinned but didn't say anything. He was too busy cutting into the layers of breaded chicken, sauce, and cheese, and devouring a hearty bite like it was the last morsel on earth. She watched the rapture on his face as he chewed and swallowed, and the eager anticipation when he dug in for more.

She followed his lead and tucked into the steaming dish in front of her. "I have to say, this really is good."

He twirled a golf ball-sized mound of spaghetti onto his fork. "I'm glad you like it."

"Where'd you learn? I mean, who taught you?"

His fork stopped mid-air. "To flirt?"

She giggled again. "No, to cook. Who taught you to cook?"

"My mother." That quick, easy smile vanished. He stared at his plate. "I used to watch her in the kitchen when I was a boy. I had three older brothers, and they were horrible. Teased me all the time. The only place I was safe was in the kitchen. I'd hide beneath this big table we had. My mother would let me stay as long as I was quiet. I would be so quiet, for hours I would sit, just watching her cut the vegetables, knead the bread, everything."

He chuckled softly at the memory, but there was a sorrow there, too. It tugged at her heart.

She touched his hand. "You must have loved her very much."

He opened his mouth to answer, but looked away instead.

She pulled her hand back. "The sauce is especially good." Maybe it was best to talk about the food. "There's so much flavor. What's in it?"

"Tomatoes, spices." He shrugged.

She slanted him a look. "So basically you're not going to tell me? Is it a family secret or something?"

This time he winked. "Or something."

"Well, it's delicious."

He nodded and took another bite.

"You're really not modest, are you?"

"Why? It's true. I make a good chicken parm. It's not bragging if it's a fact."

"Okay, smarty pants. I guess everyone has a superpower. We'll say cooking is yours."

He mulled the idea, then raised a finger. "One of my superpowers."

Was he being facetious? She couldn't tell.

"You have more than one? I can't wait to hear about the others."

"You first." He smirked and took another bite.

"What do you mean?"

He was still chewing, but that smug smile told her he was enjoying this. He swallowed. "I mean, tell me one of your superpowers." His lips twitched and she knew he was teasing her.

"So that's how it's going to be? All right, let's see." She tapped the bar top with her fingertip and thought of the possibilities. Then it came to her. "My superpower—I mean, one of my superpowers—is I can belly dance to anything. Not just Middle Eastern music, not just the usual world-fusion stuff, but anything. Jazz, classical, country, you name it."

He wrinkled his nose. "I don't believe you."

"It's true!" She bit the inside of her cheek to keep from laughing. "Ask anybody. Ask Abby."

He swiveled to face her. Something new sparked in his eyes. Something devilish. "No. Prove it."

CHAPTER TEN

TILLY SHIFTED IN HER seat and waited for that now-familiar half-smile to break Marco's stoic facade.

He didn't move.

She looked away and fidgeted with her fork. "You can't be serious."

"No?"

Now she was getting worried. Maybe a little irritated. "I spent half the night on that stage. You don't really expect me to get back up there, do you?"

Marco turned to the dark and empty platform on the other side of the room. "You danced, true. But only to music you chose."

"Yeah, but—"

"You said you could dance to anything. So dance to something I choose."

Was he for real? His blank stare told her nothing.

She threw up her hands. "Fine. If you want me to dance, I'll dance. You can pick the music, just let me finish my food."

He pinched the corners of his collar and hiked them to his jawline. "Of course. Stall as long as you like. If you take enough time, the police will arrive and you won't have to dance at all. But I'm sure that's not your intention."

How could someone so adorable be so annoying?

"No, it isn't my intention." She devoured another bite of chicken parmigiana and rose to her feet. "Let's just get this over with, shall we?" She untied the shawl around her shoulders, retied it around her hips, and made her way to the stage.

Marco followed, flipping switches to bring up the stage lights and turning knobs on the sound system, making them crackle and hum to life.

She stopped at the center of the stage. "So what's it gonna be, cowboy?"

He picked up a tablet plugged into the system and scrolled through the song list. "I don't want to make it too difficult for you."

"Don't hold back on my account. I can take whatever you dish out."

His thick, Roman brows shot up. "We'll see about that." He tapped the screen and set the tablet back on the mixer.

The hum in the speakers gave way to a familiar jingling of bells. Her chin dropped to her chest and she groaned. "Really? *Jingle Bells*?"

His lips wrestled, fighting back a smile beaming in his eyes. "You said anything."

She sighed. "Right. Fine. If you want a *Jingle Bells* belly dance, you can have a *Jingle Bells* belly dance."

She turned her back to him because there was no way in the world she was going to pull this off if she had to look at him and that arrogant smirk.

Dashing through the snow...

She began her usual *taqsim* by twisting her chest to the beat, to the right and then the left, and then rolled the movement down to her hips.

In a one horse open sleigh...

She repeated the combination in her hips, then rolled the movement back up to her chest.

With the next verse she crossed the stage with a grapevine step before dipping into a full hip circle and whipping her hair forward and back. She stole a glance his direction and caught him smiling. Not a snicker or a smirk, but a bona fide smile. She wiggled her eyebrows.

Was that a flush creeping up his cheeks?

By the end of the song, she almost wished it wasn't over.

"I told you." She strutted to the top of the stairs when the music faded. "I can dance to anything."

He shook his finger. "You aren't done. Not yet."

"No way. I proved my point."

He gave her a sad-puppy frown. "One more?"

"Fine. One."

She tried to sound annoyed, but the truth was, she didn't mind. She kind of liked the tingle she felt when he watched her, when she had his complete attention.

He swiped through the music again. What was it going to be this time? Something quick and up-tempo? Probably something bouncy that would get her shoulders and chest jiggling and her hips and thighs wiggling. He was a guy after all.

But she was wrong. The first sound out of the speaker wasn't bright or cheery or even danceable.

Bum.........bubum.........bum
Bum.........bubum.........bum

Oh, no. Every ounce of anticipation rolled up into a reeking ball of regret. This had to be the most lethargic version of *Silent Night* she'd ever heard. It had no pep, no rhythm. It didn't matter. She wasn't going to back down.

She straightened, reached out her arms, and swayed in a snake-like way, drawing out the movement to match the lethargic beat. How was she going to keep this up for an entire song?

An idea struck her. A wicked, naughty, and kinda sexy idea. Slowly, 0h-so slowly, she worked her way down the stairs to where he was leaning against the sound system.

She wasn't entirely sure about her plan until she saw the fire in his eyes and the way he gnawed his lower lip when she got close.

He wanted her.

She could see it, and it made her bolder. She shimmied up to him and made circles with her chest. Her crimson knit top brushed softly against the smooth, black cotton of his shirt.

When she looked into his wide, anxious eyes, she could see passion simmering in their depths. When she looked at his lips—his soft and tender lips—she could see them twitch with longing.

She tried to focus on the music, but her thoughts drifted, her control slipped. He was so close. She could touch his arm, his cheek, his chest. The air intoxicated her with his sweet cinnamon scent.

He watched her without saying a word, but his lips were getting closer. Closer...

She pivoted around. If he kissed her, she'd be done. She had to hold strong. Had to keep dancing. She closed her eyes and followed the music, let it guide her hips and her hands. Slowly she lifted them over her head and her hips began slow, vertical figure eights.

That's when his hands wrapped around her waist. She gasped. Surprised, but still eager for more. He pulled her closer, and his lips dragged along her bare neck and shoulders. Every inch of her exploded with sensation.

"Oh, bella." He touched the tip of his tongue along the curve of her ear.

Whatever defense she had left dissolved into the pool of those words, that touch.

She reached behind herself and grabbed the thick denim of his waistband.

He spun her around and pinned her against the wall beside the audio equipment. He stared into her eyes without a word, but the question was clear in his expression: *Do you want this?*

She answered by rising to her tiptoes and catching his lips with hers. The kiss was hot and urgent, and the flick of his tongue against hers sent a legion of lightning bolts through her, igniting every nerve and need within her.

He lifted his hands to her jaw and held her with a gentleness she didn't expect. Then he pulled away.

"Don't stop." She could hear the need in her voice, but she didn't care. She was beyond caring about anything.

He pulled her close again and kissed her quickly. In her ear, he whispered, "Come with me."

CHAPTER ELEVEN

MARCO TOLD HIMSELF there were a hundred reasons he shouldn't be leading Tilly through the Sultan's Tent bar to the dark corridor beyond the dining room and the door nearly hidden in the shadows. But he couldn't help himself. He turned the knob and pulled her close.

"It's all right." He brushed a kiss along her cheek and breathed in her warmth. "I live up there."

She tensed and stepped back. "You live here?"

A note of disbelief mingled with something else. Fear?

He searched her expression for the answer, but it was lost in the shadows.

If this was a mistake, it didn't matter. It was already too late.

He nudged her gently and she followed him up. On the upper landing, he switched on the overhead light that illuminated his studio apartment.

"What about the police?" Her eyes darted from one corner of the room to the other, taking in the kitchenette, the flat-screen television over the bookcase, the bed. "We won't hear them up here."

She was right. And it was the perfect excuse to go back downstairs, to rewind the rash decision that had brought them here.

He turned to usher her back through the doorway. The sight of her stopped him cold. Her arms wrapped around herself. Her gaze skittering around the room like a scared kitten. A desire to calm her rushed through him. A need to protect her, to comfort her. "You're safe here. See? You can see the parking lot." He drew back the curtain hiding the room's large window. Out in the misty night, the lot's lights melded into a pair of hazy orbs. Ghostly eyes that watched them from beyond.

She stepped up to the window and touched the sill. Her breath fogged the glass. "All right. I guess you're probably not a serial killer."

The remark stopped him. "What? I've been called a lot of things, but never that."

His discomfort seemed to have the opposite effect on her. A wisp of a smile tugged her cheek. "A girl can never be too careful."

Was she teasing or testing him?

"True. But what makes you so sure I'm not—?" He had to stop. He couldn't even say the words. They stuck in his throat like pieces of dry meat. He swallowed and tried again. "You know, just out of curiosity." He spied a pair of dirty socks beside his bed and kicked them under, out of view.

She wandered to the potted spruce on his table and ran a finger over the tiny string of lights and the miniature red and gold ornaments. "A serial killer wouldn't decorate for the holidays. And he certainly wouldn't stand in front of an open window facing all that"—she gestured at the sparkling city lights hugging the Newport Beach coast—"especially when the cops could show up any minute."

"Right." He tapped his temple. "Clever and beautiful. I like that."

He caught her watching him again, and it made his own gaze dart away. It was maddening how just a look from her could throw him into a tailspin. She wasn't what he'd expected. Sweet and sexy, smart and funny. If she had a flaw, he had yet to discover it. If only he'd met her before. Perhaps things could have been different.

She went to the light switch and shut it off. "That's better." If her low and sinful voice had left any room for misunderstanding, she corrected it by pressing herself against him. "It's a much better view this way, don't you think?"

"Absolutely." But he wasn't looking at the window anymore. The moonlight touched her cheeks, her nose, the curve of her lips. And those eyes. A man could lose himself in those wide, wonderful blue eyes. He looked back at the window, back at Coast Highway and the sweep of the coastline. "I'm sorry this isn't much of a place. I've thought about moving, getting something bigger. Maybe something with a balcony where the air doesn't smell of last night's special. But this has been home for a long time. I suppose I'm just used to it."

It wasn't exactly the truth. The rent was cheap, and right now he needed every penny. But there was no point in explaining that.

She took his hand and squeezed it. "It's your place. Your very own. That's more than a lot of people have."

On top of everything else, she was kind. Damn. His gaze dipped to her smooth shoulders and the red halter, tied in a droopy-loop bow at her neck. It took every ounce of self-control not to reach over and untie that bow. He pushed the urge from his thoughts and stared out the window.

What were they talking about? He couldn't remember and the silence weighed on him.

"Tell me about your place." He grabbed at the only topic he could remember. "What's it like?"

"I don't have a place. I lived with my mom before I joined the Divas. Now I'm on the road most of the time. We stay on the bus or in hotels. Mostly hotels."

"Sounds fun." He imagined the luxury accommodations she must be used to. He looked around. How poorly did his place stack up in comparison?

"Not really. It's never anything extravagant."

A curl dropped over her cheek like a drip of honey. He brushed it back behind the delicate ridge of her ear and tried to focus on her words, but he couldn't stop staring at her lips. "What do you do during the breaks? Like now?"

"Our manager owns a house in Santa Monica. He lets me crash there when I want, and I park my car there when we're away. A lot of us stay there when we're in town, or sometimes I stay with friends. This week I was with Abby."

"What about your stuff?"

"What stuff? Everything I owned fit in a few suitcases, and they were in my car."

The sadness in her voice drove a stake into his heart.

"I'm so sorry. I didn't realize." He squeezed his forehead. How could he be such an idiot? What good was sympathy when she'd just lost everything? He hadn't had much before he'd come to the States, but he remembered how it had felt leaving it all behind.

When he'd arrived in Orange County eight years before to pursue a business degree at the university, he'd been surprised by the things he'd missed from home. His family and friends, of course. But also the little things, like the leather ball with the frayed seams he kept under his bed. The one that smelled like a warm August day from all those afternoons, kicking it back and forth with his brothers in the plaza. He missed the books in his parents' library and the framed family photographs that went back generations. He missed the ugly hand-me-down lamp that sat on the desk where he'd do his homework every night and dream of how perfect life would be in the exciting country called "America."

He'd never realized how much he relied on the comfort of things and the memories they held until they were gone.

"The strange thing is, I'm not even upset about the car or the stuff anymore." She was staring at the city lights, or maybe at nothing at all. "I've been living out of suitcases for so long, I guess I'm just used to not having anything. I'm like one of those old-fashioned traveling gypsies. A modern nomad roaming the land without a home."

It wasn't sadness in her voice anymore. It was something else.

"Maybe the show is your home. Maybe that's your place."

She smiled, but it was a weak, polite smile. More for his sake than hers. "Maybe. I hadn't thought of it like that."

"You must be eager to get back to it. The tour, I mean."

She breathed a low, mournful sigh. "At least when your eyes are on the road, you're looking forward, not back. It has been a nice break, though. I wish it wasn't almost over."

"It is?"

"Pretty much. We have the show tomorrow night—tonight, technically—and then Christmas Day off, then we're back on the road."

"So soon?"

Why was he surprised? He knew she'd be leaving. He'd counted on it. Wasn't that why it was safe to bring her up here? Because for all her great qualities, the most important one—the one that truly mattered—was she'd be leaving. Between work and Maria, life was too complicated for anything else.

He caught a flash of her blue eyes, and he realized he'd been telling himself a lie.

He hadn't brought her upstairs because she was safe. It was more than that.

If only there were time…

"We're on the road a lot," she was saying. "I used to think it was so amazing to go to these new cities and dance on new stages. And it is. Usually. Or at least it was."

"Not anymore?"

She sucked in her lips and stared into the window. He stood beside her and stared, too. He waited, not pushing or controlling. Just giving her space and silence.

"The cities all start to look alike after a while," she said after a long, quiet moment, "and the stages all feel the same. I don't know. It sounds like I'm complaining, but I'm not. It's a great life, and I know I'm fortunate. I know a ton of dancers would kill to have my spot. But this week, working in Abby's studio, that was a lot of fun, too. A different kind of fun."

"Different?"

"I didn't know I could like staying in the same place for more than a few days." She chuckled softly and shook her head. "I know that sounds stupid. It's getting late, and I'm rambling."

"It doesn't sound like rambling." He wanted so badly to wrap himself around her. He shoved his fists in his back pockets instead. "It sounds like dreaming. We all need dreams."

Even if they'll never come true.

He slapped his forehead. "I'm a terrible host. I haven't even offered you anything. Do you want something to drink? I have soda, bottled water. Not exactly a great selection."

She moved away from the window and from him. She wandered past his dinette table, and stopped at the dresser. "I'll take some water." She picked up a small framed photograph. "Is this your family?"

"It is." He pulled two plastic bottles from the mini fridge.

She ran her fingers over the glass. "Look at that baby face! How old were you?"

He flushed, recalling the wide-eyed boy he'd been in that picture. The cocky kid who was going to land in California and make a fortune building a restaurant empire. "Just graduated from what you would call high school. It was taken the weekend before I left Florence to start classes here at the university. Eight years already. I can't believe it."

"You have such a big family. Are these your brothers and sisters?"

He twisted the cap off a bottle and handed it to her.

"Just brothers. The women are their wives. No, one was still a girlfriend." He pointed to the couple in the back. "That's my mom and dad."

Papa was sitting at the head of the table in the gray suit jacket he always wore for Sunday dinner. Ma was leaning beside him, her dark hair falling to her shoulder with a shot of silver along one side. She was smiling for the picture, but he could still see a glassy look from the tears she'd been shedding only moments before. Even at the airport, she was still begging him not to leave.

"You must miss them very much. Do you ever go back?"

He shook his head. "My dad passed away a couple years after this was taken. Heart attack."

She set the photo back on the dresser. It was browner than he remembered, more faded. So long ago.

He felt her eyes on him.

"I'm sorry," she said.

He could see she really was. It wasn't just something to say. Her blue eyes brimmed with emotion and the corners of her rosy lips turned up, not into a smile, but something sweet and genuine.

"I've always wondered what it would be like to have a big family. I just had my mom. And then it was just me."

She swallowed hard and her neck and her cheeks tinted pink. She shifted away, timid or embarrassed, or both. It wasn't the sort of reaction he would have expected from her. Hell, she wasn't turning out to be what he expected at all. Spunky, almost pushy one minute. Shy and hesitant the next.

Then she put down her water, walked into his arms, and surprised him again.

"I'm sorry," she whispered. "I've never been good at small talk."

"You don't have to be sorry." He forced himself to focus on her words, not the press of her chest against his or the wisps of blond curls teasing his shoulders. "It's just life."

"So sexy, and wise, too." She breathed the words onto his neck, making it damn near impossible not to take her right there. "You're really sort of amazing."

She pressed harder against him and decimated his self-control. He couldn't think about responsibilities or repercussions. He couldn't think about obligations or fears. He had one thought: her. Her legs, her fingers, her lips. He wanted to touch every inch of her, had to *feel* every part of her. He fought that primal urge until it overwhelmed him. When he couldn't stand it another moment, he scooped her into his arms and lost his fingers in her soft, blond curls.

He waited for her to back away.

She didn't.

She leaned her head back, closed her eyes, and lifted her lips. All the flirting, all the teasing, all the uncertainty vanished. His body pulsed with a need for her, and when his lips found hers and she surrendered to the urgency of his kiss, he finally knew what he'd only suspected before: He was in trouble.

Deep, difficult, probably disastrous trouble.

CHAPTER TWELVE

TILLY LAY BESIDE Marco, feeling the steady rhythm of his breath and the comforting warmth of his bare chest against her. He'd drifted off to sleep sometime after the second round of what had been even better than expected sex. Usually sleep was all she'd want, too, but tonight she couldn't keep her eyes closed.

Instead, she watched the moonlight carve shadows into the contours of the arm he draped around her and wondered why she had no desire to leave. It was usually her first thought after passion had played itself out.

This time was different.

And she didn't want anything to change it.

Not a squad car rolling up outside, with the long-overdue officer who would need questions answered and paperwork filled out about a vehicle and a pile of things that meant less to her with each passing hour.

Not a waterfront hotel room sitting empty, ready to immerse her in luxurious solitude.

Not even her own concern that she was breaking her single-most important rule. The one she'd imposed the last time she'd fallen for a guy. The last time a guy promised she was the only one. The last time a guy said he hadn't meant to lie.

That guy, it turned out, had a wife and a baby on the way back in Kansas or maybe it was Tennessee, and she still had nightmares about that Christmas Eve phone call when that wife had begged her through tears and hysterics to please, oh-God-please leave her husband alone.

She'd never considered herself the home-wrecker type, and she'd let that cheating liar know she didn't appreciate him turning her into being one.

She'd yelled and screamed and even threw a wine glass at a wall. It was an ugly scene, but the ugliest part was knowing it wasn't all his fault. She'd fallen for him too fast. Slept with him too soon. Ignored too many red flags.

The pain left her in a daze for weeks and she'd nearly gotten herself kicked out of the Divas for missing call times and flubbing cues.

That's when she'd made her promise: No more boyfriends on the road. No more heartache or heartbreak. She could play, she could tease, but she could never, ever trust.

And absolutely no more liars.

She'd kept her promise all year.

Now there was Marco. But he was so different from the guys she usually met on the road. The musicians and the roadies holed up in a hotel for a few days before they both moved on. Guys who could weave a new story at every tour stop.

He was different.

He had an address and a steady job. He had friends. He was decent and normal.

He might pretend to be a player, but it was an act. She knew players. She'd tangled with more than her fair share of them. Players didn't make midnight dinners for damsels in distress, and they didn't tear up when they talked about family.

Marco was honest and good. She could feel it.

In the darkness, her mind wandered, imagining a life where she wasn't running to the next show or away from old memories. A life where she could finally settle down and let go.

When he'd suggested the show was her home, it had wrenched something deep inside her. She wanted it to be true, but it wasn't. It never was. The Divas had been a refuge when she needed one. A built-in community of friends who shared her love of music and dance. A family that took over every part of her life.

She immersed herself in it and it had been enough.

For a while.

This week she'd watched Abby and the other dancers at the Shimmy Shop, and she could see glimmers of a new life. And then she'd met Marco, like an answer to a question she hadn't dared to ask. A gift she'd do her best to deserve.

He shifted and it was all she could do not to roll over and wrap herself around him. To mold herself against him so nothing could come between them, not even the white sheets that smelled of cinnamon and sex. She didn't know what her future would look like without the Divas, but she knew she wanted him in it.

Maybe it was the holiday or maybe it was losing everything she owned, but she'd told him things she'd never told anyone. Things she'd been afraid to say aloud, afraid to even think. And he never turned away.

She could lie in this bed above the Sultan's Tent kitchen forever, surrounded by moonlight and his soft breath beside her.

If only her bladder didn't have other ideas.

She put it off as long as she could. When it was impossible to wait another minute, she slipped carefully from beneath his arm and rose gently, but still the floor creaked. She froze.

Marco sniffed and shifted, but he didn't wake.

Damn, he was gorgeous when he slept. The dark scruff around his jaw was scruffier, and his barely tamed black hair was a tousled mess, but he was still absolutely perfect.

She padded across the room to the tiny bathroom as quietly as she could.

When she'd finished, she washed her hands and took stock of the mess in the mirror. Not terrible, but certainly not great. She scrunched and patted her curls into some semblance of order and fixed the smeared mascara beneath her eyes. That was good enough. At least when the sun finally rose, the sight of her wouldn't send him screaming back down the stairs.

On the way back to bed, her phone's buzzing stopped her. She rushed to her purse and fished it out. It was black and silent, but the buzzing continued. She looked around and saw his phone on the dresser.

Just leave it alone. Forget it.

It buzzed again.

She bit her lip and moved closer. Just to see the screen. It was already dim, but then a text message bloomed in a green bubble against the black.

She tried to look away, but it was too late. She'd seen too much. The text message wasn't English, but she recognized two words: *amore mio.*

My love.

And she'd seen the sender's name.

Maria.

She was staring at one of the bare wooden chairs but she was still seeing that message. Burned onto her brain like a cattle brand.

There could be a dozen reasons why Marco was getting declarations of love in the middle of the night from a woman named Maria. Hundreds of reasons, maybe thousands.

But her gut told her there was only one, and it didn't matter how much she wanted to pretend otherwise.

Despite what he'd told her, despite what she wanted to believe, Marco was not perfect. He'd fooled her. Not only was he a player, he was a cheat and a liar. He was exactly like the rest, and it was stupid to feel like anything that had happened that night was real. None of it was—except the gaping, ragged hole that had been her heart.

CHAPTER THIRTEEN

TILLY STOOD IN the doorway and took a long, last look at Marco.

She knew she shouldn't be angry. He hadn't said she was special. He hadn't made any promises. Hell, he hadn't given her any reason at all to think the crazy things she'd been thinking.

She'd done it all by herself.

Still, she wanted to hurl his phone and that damned text message across the room. She wanted to kick the chair and pound the wall. Because of him, she was that woman again. She was a woman who slept with another woman's man.

She pictured a sweet, innocent girl, sitting at home somewhere beside her phone, waiting for a response to her message. The image ripped through her.

She thought she'd learned from that mistake a year ago, and here she was again.

She should have known better. He'd seemed too good to be true because he *was* too good to be true. He was a bartender for chrissake. What did she expect? A miracle?

Miracles didn't happen to her. They hadn't saved her mother, and they wouldn't save her now.

How could she be so stupid? She should have known the first time he threw one of those "bellas" around like fishing bait, angling to catch some love-starved female.

She'd fallen for it like an idiot.

She wanted to scream. She wanted to throw that stupid little Christmas tree at his head. She wanted to slam the door behind her and scare him out of that annoyingly blissful sleep.

But then he shifted, and she saw his face. So peaceful, so calm. He reached his naked arm over the empty space where she'd been and grabbed the pillow where she'd rested her head. He pulled it in, squeezing it close, and despite herself, she still wished she were lying there beside him.

It made her hate him—and herself—even more.

The darkness had given way to a silvery light when Tilly stormed out of the restaurant and nearly toppled a grizzled police officer standing on the other side of the door.

Stunned, she watched him stumble and nearly drop rump first into a potted jasmine before he righted himself. He straightened to his full height, which was a good three inches below hers, and pulled the hook end of a bite-size candy cane out of his mouth.

"Officer Grant at your service, ma'am." He grabbed the candy with his left hand and rubbed the right across his barrel of a belly a few times before extending it to her to shake.

She took it, shook, and came away with a smudge of red goo on her palm.

"Sorry about that." He rubbed his hand more vigorously on his department-issued pants. "Never could resist these things. Glad they only come around once a year, know what I mean?"

"Yeah." It was impossible to be annoyed when he was so clearly embarrassed, even if he was still clutching what remained of that half-eaten candy cane like a baby with a pacifier.

"I'm here about a…" He flipped a few pages of the notepad he cradled against his chest so his fingers were still free to hold the candy. "A stolen vehicle? Would you know anything about that?"

The balancing act must have been too much because he took hold of the notepad with his page-flipping hand and tossed the remainder of the candy cane into his mouth.

She watched him chomp, pulverizing the hard candy, and nearly forgot to respond.

"Yes. I mean, unfortunately I do. It was my car."

His thick, tangled brows pulled together. "So sorry, Miss. That is a downright shame."

A few minutes later, she'd told him everything he needed to know to fill in the blanks on his form and itemized a list of things that had been inside the car.

His brows squeezed across his red, bulbous nose. "That's quite a few belongings you had with you. A lot of temptation for the unsavory sort, if you know what I mean. Especially this time of year."

She dug her toe into a crevice in the pavement. She could tell him it was everything she owned in the world. Every stitch of clothing. Every piece of jewelry. Every hairpin. Every family picture and memento from her childhood. Even her mother's death certificate. It was all there, in the back of that little car.

But it didn't matter. It was just stuff.

"Yeah, I should have been more careful." She stared at the steel-gray clouds hanging low over the coast and the cars whizzing by. It couldn't be much past six-thirty and already there were so many people wide awake and on their way to the places they needed to be. She should have been one of them. There was a hotel room with her name on it, sitting empty and waiting.

She glanced up at the window she knew was Marco's. No light, no movement. He was probably still sleeping, oblivious to everything.

Angry talons gripped her chest.

Get through this and get out of here.

"Are we finished?" She regretted the sharpness in her voice. It wasn't Officer Grant's fault her life sucked.

He didn't seem to notice. He licked his thumb and flipped through his notebook. He nodded, ripped out a yellow carbon-copy page, and handed it to her. He hesitated, then reached into his top breast pocket. He pulled a candy cane out and handed it to her. "Want one?"

She shook her head. "Do you think there's any chance you'll find my car or my stuff?"

He broke the wrapping on the red and white candy himself and stuck it in his mouth. "There's always a chance," he said, his lips maneuvering around the candy. "We'll just have to see."

But the way he said it and the way he shrugged when he shuffled back to his squad car told her not to get her hopes up.

CHAPTER FOURTEEN

IT WAS NEARLY noon by the time Tilly climbed into her rented red coupe with the paper floor mats and the new car smell. It had taken one app-ordered car ride, four calls to her insurance company, and three hours on a plastic chair in the rental shop lobby in the dingiest part of the city, but she had wheels again and the promise of an insurance company reimbursement, even if her nerves were frazzled to the core.

Just get to the hotel.

It was the mantra that had gotten her through those hours and the one that kept away any thought of…

No. She couldn't think of him. Not now. Not ever again.

She pointed the car's nose toward the beach and drove toward the perfect view of the Pacific from her abandoned hotel room. Her perfect getaway, her perfect holiday for one.

Golden sunshine had burned away the morning clouds and left the sky a brilliant crystal blue. That shameless sun that might look out of place anywhere else on Christmas Eve was bearing down on her and her new ride, warming all her cold places and brightening all the dark ones. All the crazy thoughts she'd had last night—about leaving the Divas and settling down—that was gone, too. She chocked it up to too many drinks and too little sleep. There had been plenty of romantic, holiday notions thrown into the mix, too, but it didn't matter. She was back to her senses now.

By the time she pulled into the hotel's self-parking lot, she was ready to get back to her plan: crawl into a cocoon of luxury sheets, get to the theater for curtain, come back and crawl into that cocoon again until she had to be at the airport. A day and a half of rest, relaxation, and a ridiculous amount of room service.

When she opened the door to her room, the beauty of the sparkling ocean greeted her through the wall-to-wall sliding glass doors. Oh, that view! She ignored the meticulously made king-size bed, the designer armoire, and the matching desk and walked directly out to the narrow balcony overlooking the hotel pool and a panoramic view of Newport Bay, filled with yachts and sailboats and lined with multi-million-dollar mansions.

She closed her eyes and inhaled the saltwater air and the sunshine. She took it all in—the squawk of sea gulls, the brush of the breeze across her cheeks, the lapping of the water against the docks. It was paradise, and everything she'd hoped.

At least it was until she heard another sliding glass door open. A couple appeared on the next balcony over. They might have noticed her, too, but it was impossible to tell because they seemed to be enjoying each other far more than the view, if all the cooing and kissing was any indication.

She slipped quietly back inside and pulled down the soft and fluffy-as-a-cloud comforter and the luxury sheets. She kicked off her shoes, slid into the opening, and pulled the covers up to her chin. If heaven were a bed, it would feel like this. She closed her eyes and snuggled in. She turned on her side. She turned on her other side. She flopped on her back. Her eyes popped open.

Okay, so sleep wasn't in her near future. She was a little hungry, though. She slid out of the bed and picked up the phone.

"Room service, please."

The attendant connected her and after another series of rings, another attendant picked up.

"Good afternoon, Miss Bennett. How may I help you?"

His formality surprised her, but only for a moment.

"Do you have something like a chicken sandwich?"

"Club or salad?"

"Club."

"Anything else?"

"Bottled water?"

"Of course. A chicken club sandwich and a bottled water."

"Do you have ice cream?"

If this was going to be her Christmas escape, there had to be ice cream.

"Yes. Chocolate, strawberry, and vanilla."

"Can I get a little of all three?"

"Certainly, Miss Bennett."

If there was a note of judgment in his voice, she chose to ignore it.

She hung up and found a wide screen television hidden in the armoire. She turned it on with the remote on the nightstand, slid back into bed, and settled in for a movie marathon.

She flipped past news channels, children's channels, home improvement channels. One movie looked promising, until she realized it was *Miracle on 34th Street*. Click. The next one was a Santa flick starring a guy from an 1980s sitcom. Click. Every movie turned out to be a Christmas movie.

No, thank you.

She settled on a home improvement channel, where a guy was in the crawlspace under a house pointing out inspection problems with his flashlight. It wasn't ideal, but it wasn't a deal breaker until she had to turn up the volume to cover the sound of bedsprings and a backboard knocking against the wall.

She considered knocking on the door. Yeah, that wasn't going to happen.

She could call the front desk and complain. No way.

She picked up the phone and dialed.

"Hello, Miss Bennett. How can I help you?"

"Please cancel my room service order. I've decided to go out."

CHAPTER FIFTEEN

THE SHIMMY SHOP'S bell jingled when Tilly walked through the door.

"I'm back here."

Abby's distant voice seemed to be coming from the dance room down the hall, so that's where Tilly headed, dodging scattered folding chairs and used paper plates that hadn't quite made it to the trash bin. Is this how they'd left the place last night? Why hadn't Abby asked for help? Why hadn't Tilly offered?

Suddenly, her plan to ask for the dance room for some solo practice seemed inexcusably selfish.

She stuck her head into the room and found Abby folding the white plastic chairs and stacking them in a corner. "Hey, I came to help. I hope I'm not too late."

"You didn't have to do that." Abby dropped another chair on the stack and wiped her forehead. "But I'm glad you did. I could use the company."

"Tell me what I can I do."

Abby grabbed another chair. "You can start by telling me what happened last night. I thought you were going to your aunt's, but since you haven't changed…" She gave Tilly a long, knowing look.

Tilly looked down at her red halter and black skirt. She'd completely forgotten about her clothes. "That was the plan, but my car was stolen and, well—"

Abby dropped a chair. It clattered on the floor. "Marco didn't say anything about your car."

Instantly, the room's temperature shot up thirty degrees.

"Marco?" She nearly choked on his name.

Abby picked up the chair again and muscled it to the stack, making her waist-length ponytail swing and bounce behind her. "Yeah. He called this morning, looking for you."

"He did?" Tilly glanced down. Flames crept up her cheeks.

Abby grabbed another chair and leaned against it. "I figured you guys hooked up. But he must have been worried about you, or wondering about your car. Are you all right?"

"I'm fine. What did he say?"

"Nothing about your car. I can't believe he didn't say anything."

"Yeah, but what *did* he say?"

Abby frowned. "He said, 'I need to talk to Tilly.' That was it. It wasn't complicated."

Not complicated? She had no idea. But why would he call Abby? Was he angry? Was he feeling guilty? If he wanted to get the message to her that it had all been a mistake, he didn't have to bother.

Abby crossed her arms and cocked her head to the side. She knew something was up. "So there was something to all those sparks flying between you two?"

"Hardly." She tried to force a laugh but it sounded like a sputter. "We killed some time last night, that's all. I guess that's the best way to put it. It was nothing."

Abby's mouth twisted. "That wasn't the impression I got. He was pretty insistent, now that I think about it."

Why? So he could spew more lies. No, thank you.

Tilly folded a chair and added it to the stack. "Look, I know he's your friend, but that guy is a creep."

Abby straightened.

"I found out the hard way," Tilly added. "He's a player and a cheater."

"A cheater? But he doesn't have a girlfriend."

"Believe me, I was surprised, too. But I saw it for myself."

"You saw his girlfriend?"

"I saw her text message on his phone. I wasn't trying to be nosy, but the screen was right in front of my face. I don't know Italian, but I know what *amore mio* means."

Saying the words out loud gave her a sick feeling.

"What did he say about it?"

"He didn't say anything. He was asleep, so I got out of there."

"Then how do you know it was his girlfriend?" Abby scratched her forehead. "Couldn't there be another explanation?"

For a sharp, business-savvy woman, Abby could really be dumb.

"Who else could it be? He doesn't have any sisters and his mom died."

"He told you that?"

"I know, right?" Tilly smirked. "Not exactly the best pickup line ever, but it worked. I told him about my mom, and he told me about his. It doesn't matter. It's over. Moving on. Look, I didn't come to spill my sob story to you. Just let me help you clean up. Tell me what I can do."

She noticed two plastic garbage bins in the center of the dance room filled to the brim with discarded paper cups and plates, bottles, and cans. Two long tables were folded and leaning against the wall, and most of the chairs were as well.

Abby scanned the room. "I know it looks like a lot, but once the rental company comes to pick up the chairs and tables, I'm practically done." Her lips wrestled with a thought. "But if you aren't terribly busy, there is something you could do to help. I mean, if you don't mind."

"Sure. Name it."

Abby pointed to a row of vases holding red roses and white tiger lilies lined up against the wall. "I promised a friend I'd donate those to a nursing home on the bay. They're having a party tonight for the residents and their families, and they were hoping to get them by two. I didn't think it would be a problem, but now the rental company is running late and I can't leave."

It was already half past one. If she hit green lights the entire way, she might get there by two. But she also needed to get to a store to replace some essentials before the show and get to the theater on time.

Abby noticed the hesitation and amped up the sad-puppy act. "I'd *really* appreciate it, if you could do it."

After giving her a place to crash for a week and everything else she'd done, how could she say no? "Of course I'll do it. What's the address?"

Abby wrote it on a sticky note and handed it over. "When you get there, ask for Mrs. Rizzetti. That's really important, okay?"

"Rizzetti. Got it. Anything else?"

Abby shook her head. "That should take care of everything."

CHAPTER SIXTEEN

TILLY DIDN'T HIT a single green light on the way down Newport Boulevard, and parking proved an even bigger challenge. She lapped the block three times before a street-side spot opened up within reasonable walking distance of Newport Horizons, a luxury assisted-living facility off the bay's main channel. When she finally entered the reception lobby, lugging a vase in each arm, she was seriously wishing she had suggested she wait for the rental company instead.

The woman behind the receptionist desk didn't seem to notice. She was too busy brushing lint from her mauve knit jacket and matching skirt. When she finally did notice Tilly, she dropped the lint brush on the desk, lifted a pair of eyeglasses hanging on a beaded chain around her neck, and slid them up her tiny, pinched nose.

"Oh, what lovely arrangements. And who are these for, dear?"

"I believe they're for a party tonight. I'm supposed to deliver them to Mrs. Rizzetti."

The woman's glazed-eye smile dropped. "Did you say Mrs. *Rizzetti?*"

Damn. She'd probably mispronounced the name. She should have had Abby write it down. "Abby Anderson from the Shimmy Shop sent me. She said Mrs. Rizzetti would be expecting them. I have four more in my car."

The woman still looked confused, but she was trying her best to be gracious. "We have been expecting flowers from Miss Anderson. But Mrs. Rizzetti... Oh, it doesn't matter. Let me get you some help."

She walked to a window behind the desk where the shutters were pulled open. Behind it was a room filled with staff in nursing scrubs arranging banquet tables and chairs in a space already decked out with holiday decor. She leaned through the window. "Stephanie? May I trouble you?"

A young woman with a bun pulled high on her head looked up from where she was positioning a forest green tablecloth over a table. "Certainly, Dr. Foster."

A moment later Stephanie joined them in the lobby.

"The arrangements have arrived." Dr. Foster gestured at Tilly. "Could you help this young lady to bring them in?"

"Of course. Here, let me get those for you." Stephanie relieved Tilly of the two vases she was holding and disappeared around the corner. She returned empty-handed. "Where'd you park?"

Tilly led her out of the building and down the street a half-block to the metered parking spot she'd nabbed in front of a closed maritime antique store. She popped the rental car's trunk.

"Oh, these are incredible." Stephanie leaned into the space and inhaled. "They smell heavenly. The residents are going to love them." She grabbed a vase in each arm. "A big improvement over the dusty silk arrangements we usually pull out of storage."

"Sounds like it's going to be a fun party." Tilly grabbed the remaining two vases and closed the trunk.

"It's not much, really. There's never enough in the budget to do everything we'd like, but the residents enjoy themselves. They dress up, we sing carols, and we usually hire some kind of entertainment."

"What? Like a mall Santa?"

Stephanie giggled. "No, not Santa. This year it was supposed to be Victorian carolers. A husband and wife team who wear period costumes and sing, but they canceled this morning. He has pneumonia. His wife was so sweet. She offered to come on her own, but we told her it was best if she stayed home and took care of him. Some of our residents are very sensitive to the bugs that go around this time of year, so we need to be really careful."

"That's too bad."

"The party will be a little quieter this year, but we'll manage. We have a good stereo for holiday music. Maybe we'll do a sing-along, and the more active ones will undoubtedly want to dance. Mrs. Rizzetti, I heard you mention her to the director, she's especially light on her feet. During her better moments, anyway."

Tilly stopped. "Mrs. Rizzetti is a resident?"

"Didn't you know?"

When they had delivered the bouquets to the banquet room, Tilly returned to the lobby to find Dr. Foster talking with a small, roundish woman whose warm chestnut eyes crinkled when she smiled.

"Mrs. Rizzetti," Dr. Foster said, "may I introduce… oh dear, I didn't get your name."

"I'm Tilly. Tilly Bennett."

"*Meravigliosa!*" the older woman whispered and clapped her hands to her chest.

The director leaned closer to Mrs. Rizzetti. "This is the young woman I told you about." She spoke slowly, carefully enunciating each word. "She brought those lovely flowers—*fiori*—for our banquet." She pointed through the window to the vases.

Mrs. Rizzetti took Tilly's hand. "*Grazie mille, cara, sono bellisimi.* Come."

Before Tilly knew what was happening, the woman had a grip on her and was pulling her toward the hallway. She looked back at the director and Stephanie. Both stood, frozen, their eyes glazed in surprise or alarm, or both.

"Mrs. Rizzetti?" the director called. "Mrs. Rizzetti, I'm sure the young lady can't stay."

Mrs. Rizzetti didn't turn around. She didn't even slow down. She only wagged her finger in the air and repeated, "*Un attimo, un attimo.*"

When Mrs. Rizzetti turned a corner, Tilly lost sight of the director. She could have wrestled out of Mrs. Rizzetti's grasp, but the woman was so determined. So focused on getting somewhere. And despite the hour and all the things she needed to do before tonight's performance, she couldn't help but wonder: Where were they going?

CHAPTER SEVENTEEN

TILLY FOLLOWED MRS. Rizzetti deep into the assisted-care facility, down wallpapered corridors with slick linoleum floors and polished chrome railings. At the elevator, they stopped beside a resident in a pink terrycloth robe standing beside a rolling, intravenous drip. The up button was alight, but Mrs. Rizzetti tapped it anyway.

Tilly turned to the resident with the IV and found the woman staring, lifelessly, in her direction. She turned away but not before a shiver raced down her spine. She glanced down the hallway. Nothing. She turned back. Nothing there, either. Just the tinny and maudlin instrumental music piped through the speakers.

This was obviously a mistake. Her heart thundered against her ribs. Her fingers twitched. It was the hospital all over again.

When the elevator doors slid open, she stumbled back.

"Come, come." Mrs. Rizzetti patted Tilly's hand and tugged her forward.

An overwhelming desire to flee was held in check only by her fear of offending this sweet woman. She looked so happy, so harmless. Really, how threatening could she be?

On the ride up, Tilly stared at the numbers above the door and felt her pulse quicken. Two, three. The elevator stopped and the woman in the robe walked off with her IV drip. The doors closed, the elevator rose again, and Tilly gripped the railing so hard her knuckles hurt. Four, five, six. The top floor.

The compartment lurched to a stop, and her knees turned to cooked noodles. Shadows rushed in from the periphery. Flashes from that horrible night in the emergency room. The blue paper masks and shower caps. The flickering fluorescent light. The buzzes, beeps, and whooshes from the machine smothering her mother in tubes and hoses.

Leave.

Now.

But when the doors split apart, it was an entirely different place. No linoleum. No wallpaper. No anguish.

An ocean of blue carpet welcomed her into a cozy lobby painted the color of crisp morning sun. A polished colonial cabinet offered a crystal bowl of green apples and bottles of French sparkling water beside a giant Boston fern.

Mrs. Rizzetti tugged her again, urging her along the hallway, passing door after door until she stopped at one. The old woman turned the unlocked knob.

Tilly peered over the woman's head, with its single streak of silver hair that started over her right eyebrow and disappeared into a tight black chignon. Inside, she could see a quaint little apartment filled with elegant furnishings. A Victorian-style settee, wooden occasional tables, a formal dining set. It would have looked like something out of the nineteenth century if there hadn't also been a giant gray recliner facing a giant LED screen television.

Tilly sniffed. "Is that gingerbread?" The words were already out when she remembered the woman didn't speak English.

Mrs. Rizzetti, who was already in and removing the chiffon scarf from around her neck and hanging it on a hook beside the door, smiled at her. "Yes, actually. But do please come in. Don't be shy. I had a feeling you might enjoy a nibble."

The look on her face must have given away her shock.

Mrs. Rizzetti's eyes twinkled. "Yes, dear, I do speak English." She touched her finger to her lips and shut the door. "But it shall be our secret, *no?*"

Tilly choked on a laugh. "Okay. But why?"

"It makes my life easier. Maybe I don't hear? Maybe I don't answer? They leave me alone. Go on, sit. I will get the cookies."

The woman shuffled into the kitchen. Tilly moved to the sliding glass door. Below, hundreds of gazillion-dollar mansions sat side-by-side, most of them linked to docks with equally impressive yachts. In the distance, Coast Highway snaked along the coastline. The same stretch of Coast Highway she'd watched last night, before...

She squeezed her eyes shut and pushed the thought away.

Forget him. Forget all of it.

She opened her eye and turned her back on the window, the view, everything.

"Can I do anything to help?"

She could see the woman in the kitchen, standing beneath an open cabinet door and stretching to reach a shelf of teacups.

"Just tell me, dear, tea or coffee?" Her finger hooked around a tiny, curved handle and she pulled down what looked like a bone china teacup and then its matching saucer. She set it beside another already on the counter.

"Neither, thank you. I really can't stay."

"*Tsk-tsk-tsk*. Young people, always in such a hurry."

Why did she feel guilty? The woman had practically kidnapped her. Still, she couldn't ignore the silence or that stare.

"I have a show to do tonight, and I still have to get ready."

"Oh! A show? What kind, dear?"

"I'm a dancer."

The woman's hands shot to her chest. "I should have known. I dreamed of being a ballerina once. Long ago. Before my husband. Before the children." She pointed at Tilly. "Ballerina?"

Tilly shook her head. "Belly dancer." She braced for the inevitable frown and flustered attempt to change the subject that she'd come to expect after telling a stranger about her profession.

Instead, the woman brightened.

"Oh, I love the belly dancing," she gushed. "My son works at a restaurant where there is belly dancing. I beg him to take me, but he's so old-fashioned. A— how do you say it? oh, yes—a stick in the mud. Let me get the kettle going. We will have tea."

"All right." She really did need to be going. There were so many things to do, makeup that needed replacing, the usual toiletries to get her through the next few days. But she was already here. She may as well have a little tea with those delicious smelling cookies.

Mrs. Rizzetti disappeared back into the kitchen and Tilly walked along a wall filled with a dozen framed photographs. There were faded images of a young woman with pin-curl bangs and a shy smile that must have been Mrs. Rizzetti in her youth. Another of that same young woman with a dapper, raven-haired man in a military uniform. There were children, babies and toddlers and teens. One photograph caught her eye. It was recent, a sunset shot taken along a popular stretch of Laguna Beach. It was Mrs. Rizzetti, her eyes bright and proud, under the arm of a young man with jet black hair, a scruff along his chin, and familiar, piercing brown eyes.

The resemblance between the two hit her like an electric shock.

"What's the name of the restaurant where your son works?" Had her voice trembled? Her throat was so dry, her tongue like cotton.

Mrs. Rizzetti was arranging the cups onto a tray. "The Tent. No, the Sultan. I don't know. Something like that."

A coil squeezed around her chest. "The Sultan's Tent?"

"Yes! You know it?" The woman emerged from the kitchen, carrying a tray with two teacups and a pot nestled beneath a crocheted cozy. "Then you must know my son, Marco. That's him." Mrs. Rizzetti was beside her, pointing to the young man in the picture. "That's my Marco. So handsome, so good. He is my angel."

CHAPTER EIGHTEEN

MRS. RIZZETTI RATTLED off something in Italian Tilly didn't understand, but it didn't matter. She couldn't move. She couldn't breathe.

The pieces were falling into place. It was the reason she was here, why Abby had sent her and insisted she ask for this woman.

"You would like him," Mrs. Rizzetti continued. "Such a sweet boy. Always a gentleman. I don't know what I'd do without him." She began to hum to herself and to sway, and then the tray slipped from her fingers and crashed onto the coffee table. Tea and tiny ceramic shards shot out across the living room in every direction.

Mrs. Rizzetti stared with wide, astonished eyes at the broken pieces and the puddle of tea at her feet.

Tilly navigated through the shards and touched the woman's shoulder. "Are you all right?"

In that instant the spell broke. Tears welled in Mrs. Rizzetti's eyes. She murmured "*Oh, mamma, mi dispiace, mi dispiace, mamma*" again and again.

Instinctively, Tilly wrapped her arms around the woman and guided her away from the mess to a chair. "It's all right, Mrs. Rizzetti. Sit here, I'll clean up."

The woman buried her face in her hands and sobbed like a schoolgirl. Her chest shuddered. Tilly bent down and cradled the gentle curve of the woman's shoulders and rocked with her.

When the sobbing eased, Tilly stood. "I'm going to clean up now. Don't worry about anything. I've got this."

Mrs. Rizzetti said nothing. Instead, she rocked, back and forth, back and forth, and stared and her hands clasped in her lap.

"Ma'am, are you all right?"

Still the woman didn't meet her glance, or even acknowledge the question.

Tilly stepped back, waiting for Mrs. Rizzetti to snap back to life. Fearing what to do if she didn't.

Nothing changed. The woman swayed. Her lips moved, but no sound came out and she showed no sign of acknowledging Tilly at all.

Panicked, Tilly found the phone on a doily on a pedestal table. Her finger aimed at nine, but there was another button. A red one labeled "emergency." She pressed it.

Five minutes later, Dr. Foster and two uniformed orderlies were in the apartment.

The young men hovered over Mrs. Rizzetti. One administered a shot into her upper arm, another took her temperature. Dr. Foster mopped up the tea.

She approached Tilly when she was done. "Maria usually does well during the day. It's when night falls that she has her troubles." She tugged at the wrists of her knit blazer to straighten her sleeves. "It's good you were here. She might have hurt herself if she were alone. So, thank you."

Tilly didn't want to be thanked. Her brain was still locked on what Dr. Foster had said. That name she'd used. "Maria?"

Dr. Foster grinned. "Pardon me. I should say Mrs. Rizzetti."

Maria Rizzetti.

The name changed everything. Already she'd been sitting, sifting through the things Marco had said about his mother. About the sadness. About the heartbreak. Only it wasn't in his past, as he'd led her to believe. It was now. It was over and over again. She'd lost her mother in a moment. He was watching his slip away, a little further every day.

And now to discover this: Maria wasn't a girlfriend. She was his mother.

He wasn't a cheat. He wasn't a player.

If only she could rewind time. If only she could crawl back into bed—his bed—and undo everything.

All she wanted was to be back in his arms.

"*Grazie, bella.*"

Her head shot up. Mrs. Rizzetti was standing in front of her, smiling. The woman glanced to where Dr. Foster was chatting with the orderlies, lowered her voice, and took Tilly's hand in hers. "I am so sorry about all this. I hope I didn't frighten you."

"I'm not frightened. Just worried about you. Are you all right?"

"*Sì, sì,* right as rain. But you, bella, you look like you've seen a ghost."

Tilly straightened. "No, I'm all right. I think I'll be all right. I just realize there's something I have to do."

"What, dear?"

She held Mrs. Rizzetti's tiny, fragile hand. "Would you come to my show tonight? I would love to have you there as my guest. And you could bring your son."

"Marco? Well, I don't know. We have the party, but... Never mind, yes. I accept. It would be a wonderful surprise for him."

That's certainly what Tilly was hoping for.

Mrs. Rizzetti shuffled to the kitchen and packed a small plate of gingerbread cookies, some shaped as stars, others as bells and wreaths, all piped with shiny white icing.

Tilly followed her She spoke softly. "I'll leave tickets under your name at will call. It's Mrs. Maria Rizzetti, right?"

Mrs. Rizzetti glanced at Dr. Foster across the room. The woman was watching them now. Mrs. Rizzetti turned back to Tilly.

"*Sì, bella,*" she said. "*Grazie.*"

CHAPTER NINETEEN

TILLY PEEKED THROUGH the backstage door at the audience streaming into the theater. The burgundy velvet seats were filling fast, but not all of them. And not 5C and 6C. The orchestra-level pair sat empty, alone, rejected.

"Where are they?" Her fingertips drummed against the dull black door. What was left of her frayed hope leached into its hard, cold metal.

Was it already too late? Was he too angry to forgive her?

The thought of seeing him had propelled her through the day, easing the inconvenience of having to dart around town to replace some essentials before the show and the occasional bouts of self-pity. It was only a car. An old beater of a car at that. And it was just stuff. Mostly stupid, who-cares-anyway stuff.

But it was her stuff. It was all she had.

Never mind.

What was the point of dwelling on the past? Look forward. Move forward.

That's what she'd told herself all day, and that's what she was trying to do.

She was going to make things right with Marco. That's what mattered.

But where was he?

Her heart pounded like a wrecking ball inside her chest. Her fingers curled until her nails bit deep into her flesh. She wanted to scream and kick the door and forget she'd ever set eyes on that man.

"There you are!"

Her breath caught in her throat at the sound of the familiar voice behind her. It was Melanie, in full makeup and costume.

"We've been looking everywhere for you." Melanie tapped a button on her phone and put it to her ear. "Found her. Yeah. We'll be right there."

"What's the problem? It's not curtain time yet." The words shot out like poison darts.

Melanie tapped a button on the phone and backed away like someone backing away from a wild animal.

"We've got about two minutes. We're lining up. "

"Just two?" She glanced back through the sliver of space at the seats. Still empty.

"Who are you looking for?" Melanie peered over her shoulder.

"It doesn't matter. They didn't come."

She looked away so Melanie wouldn't see the tears welling in her eyes.

Melanie patted her back. "Don't feel bad. It's Christmas Eve. People have obligations and all kinds of things going on. It could be anything. Don't take it personally."

"I know. You're right." But she knew the truth. It didn't matter if it was Christmas Eve or the last day on earth. Marco didn't want to see her.

On stage, she waited for the music to wash away the pain. To free her of her thoughts and her worries. Her regrets. Usually the melody and the movement lifted her out of herself, freeing her from everything that weighed her down. She waited for that moment tonight.

It never came.

At the end of the set, when the stage lights changed and she could glimpse the audience, she searched the shadows again. She found the same thing. Two empty seats. Dual reminders that actions have consequences and mistakes can't always be fixed.

She knew there would be no second chance.

She knew something else, too: She couldn't ignore her heart anymore. She couldn't pretend this was the life she wanted just because it was the life she chose. The traveling, the non-stop work, the excuse not to have a real life.

She wanted something different. Something more. She'd known it last night, lying in Marco's arms. But it was still true now.

She needed a change.

She stepped off the stage after the applause, and she knew it was the last time.

As if on cue, Garrett was in the wings, watching. A smile on his face, but that wasn't going to make it any easier.

She grabbed a towel and a bottled water an assistant handed to her, took a breath, and walked up to him.

"Do you have a minute?"

He eyed her with suspicion. "Do I have a choice?"

She swallowed hard and wiped at the perspiration accumulating on her forehead, knowing it had nothing to do with the performance and everything to do with the warning in his steel-gray eyes.

"No, you don't. We need to talk."

CHAPTER TWENTY

MARCO STOOD AT the window overlooking Newport Bay and tried again to make his mother see reason.

"You don't even know her." He stared at the lights gleaming into the night sky from the multi-million-dollar mansions and the yachts that populated the channel, but his mind was somewhere else. "Tonight's your Christmas party. You've been looking forward to it for weeks. You bought a new dress."

"No, *figlio mio*. You bought the dress." She emerged from her bedroom wearing the red silk charmeuse gown they'd picked out together the weekend before. She fussed with the collar's closure. "I told you I didn't need anything new. I could have made do with something in my closet."

He went to her and helped her with the button. "You deserve a new dress. I told you it was a Christmas present. I want my mother to feel special on this special day."

"You already do too much. You should save your money for your restaurant."

"Don't worry. There's enough." Enough to cover his portion of his mother's living expenses, her medical expenses, his own rent. Not much more. But she didn't need to know that. When she was diagnosed last year, he'd been ready to move back to Italy to help and be near her. It had surprised him and his brothers that her only request was to move to Southern California to be with him.

His brothers blamed it on the postcards of palm trees and seaside sunsets he'd been sending since college. "Marco's paradise," she called it.

Since she'd arrived, she was his only concern. He tried to live every day like it might be her last, because sometimes, during her worst episodes, it seemed as though it would be. It didn't frighten him anymore. He played along when she thought she was a child again and he was her brother, or her father, or any number of people she plucked from her earliest memories. She always snapped out of it, eventually. Lately, however, the episodes were more frequent and she didn't have the same energy.

Her doctors said it was a sign the medications were losing the battle.

It wasn't what he wanted to hear.

"The tickets were going to be my Christmas present to you."

His head tipped back, and he sighed. Why wouldn't she let the topic drop? He never wished for her memory lapses, but it wouldn't be the worst thing if this invitation was lost in one of those voids.

"I could just as easily wear this dress to the show."

Her voice hiked up a notch. She wasn't going to let this go.

Ignoring her wasn't going to work, either. It never did. He'd have to try something else.

"That was a very nice thought." He used his sweet voice. His I-may-be-your-baby-but-I-know-what's-best voice. He took her small, fragile hands. "I appreciate it, but I already have the very best gift. I have my mother."

"Oh, stop it." She batted him away but she was grinning, maybe even blushing. "I must be honest, though. There was another reason I wanted to go. I wanted you to meet the young lady. She's a lovely girl and about your age. I think you would like her."

His lips pinched, caging the question he still wanted answered. But if he asked his mother how it was that Tilly Bennett had managed to become her new best friend in one afternoon—and this afternoon in particular—there would be no stopping the torrent of questions it would set off.

He suspected he already knew the answer anyway. It had been a mistake to call the Shimmy Shop. When he'd awakened to the empty bed and the empty parking lot, none of it made sense. Why would she leave without saying goodbye? Why would she leave at all?

After a shower, a cup of coffee, and that unfortunate conversation with Abby, it was clear. He hadn't been the only one looking for temporary companionship last night. And even though he'd changed his mind, it was clear Tilly Bennett had not.

CHAPTER TWENTY-ONE

THE NEWPORT HORIZON'S lobby was not the same place Tilly had left a few hours earlier. Tinseled garland and cotton ball snow had transformed every surface. Stuffed santas and stacks of wrapped gifts filled the bookshelves. Even the lazy instrumentals pumped through the speakers were replaced with cheerful Christmas carols. It was cute and quaint and quite welcoming, except for the foam-core poster dripping in red and green glitter acknowledging in large, hand-drawn letters "Our Dear Friends and Family."

It stopped her cold.

Her lips rolled inward. She wasn't a friend. She wasn't family. She wasn't anything, and maybe this whole thing was a mistake.

The confidence that had propelled her down Newport Boulevard seeped out of her like air from a punctured balloon.

Down the corridor, high heels clicked on the linoleum floor. She couldn't face the director. She couldn't face anybody.

She pivoted and hurried to the door.

"Oh, good! You're already here."

The voice was light, happy, and definitely not the director. It was Stephanie, out of her nurse scrubs and in a winter white party dress with a silk poinsettia brooch at her left shoulder. Her cheeks, tucked up in a smile, were framed by loose curls that bounced with each step.

"Dr. Foster was thrilled to get your call. She asked me to be sure you have anything you need. Can I get you something to drink? A room where you can change?" She looked up at the top bookshelf and frowned. "What happened to Rudolph? I know I set him there this afternoon." She walked to the shelf, rose on her tiptoes, and patted the fluffy white cotton. "There you are. Lost in the snow."

Tilly had Stephanie by a few inches and she could see the reindeer legs the woman was groping for. She stepped up. "I can do that for you."

"No, that's—"

The sound of fabric tearing stopped her. Her arm shot down, but it was too late. Stephanie craned her neck to see the damage, but it was tucked behind her shoulder, out of view. Tilly could see it, though. Two gaping inches of bare flesh where the sleeve's seam should be.

"Is it bad?" Panic edged Stephanie's voice. "Please don't let it be bad. It isn't my dress."

"It isn't ... terrible."

Tilly's halfhearted response didn't fool Stephanie.

"It was an accident," Tilly said, trying to calm her. "I'm sure she'll understand. It's nothing a few safety pins won't fix."

"But it's her dress. It probably costs more than I make in a month."

"Oh." Tilly pinched her lip. She had an idea. Not a great idea, but it was something.

"I could fix it for you."

Stephanie patted at the area, feeling the size of the problem. "How? Are you hiding a sewing machine in that bag?" She gestured at Tilly's tote, one of her afternoon purchases.

"No, but I have a sewing kit." She pulled out a little blue box containing a pair of mini scissors, a needle, three tiny spools of thread, and a few safety pins. Her usual kit was nicer and better equipped, but considering the kind of luck she was having lately, she knew she'd better grab whatever she could before trying to take the stage tonight. "It'll just take a few minutes. It won't be perfect, but it'll work."

"Are you kidding? You're a lifesaver."

Tilly looked around. "Is there someplace we can go? A room?"

Stephanie pointed to a closed door off to the left. "That's Dr. Foster's office. She won't mind."

They went inside and Stephanie shut the door. "Where do you want me to stand?"

"Anywhere. Just give me the dress." Tilly pushed aside the writing pad and ballpoint pen on Dr. Forster's desk to make room for her tote. She pulled out the white thread, a needle, and the scissors. When she looked up to get the dress, Stephanie was staring at her with fear in her eyes.

Tilly held out her hand. "The dress?"

"Can't I keep it on?"

That panicked look took Tilly back to the first time she was asked to share a dressing room with twenty other dancers. It had rattled her more than the performance. "Here." She unbuttoned the trench coat that covered her from neck to knee and handed it to Stephanie. "I'll turn around. You can wear this till I'm done."

"Thanks."

But Stephanie wasn't looking at the coat. She was staring at Tilly.

"That's an incredible costume."

Tilly looked down at the snug scarlet gown with its peek-a-boo midriff, lace, beads, and sequins. "Thanks. It's one of my favorites." And thanks to her new coat, the Divas' costume manager hadn't noticed her leave without checking it back in.

Stephanie touched the lace sleeve. "It looks more like an evening gown than, I don't know, something you'd see in *Arabian Nights*. The lace is especially nice."

Tilly touched the lace, too. "I like it, too."

When she'd gone to the fitting and seen the designer's mock-up in solid, glossy Lycra, it had looked like a giant fishing lure. She'd suggested adding the stretch lace to give it a softer, more feminine appeal onstage. She'd also suggested a tapered length and a more modest leg slit, but those ideas had been ignored.

That wouldn't happen again.

She took Stephanie's dress and went to work.

Five minutes later, she tied off the thread and snipped away the remainder. She shook out the dress and examined the seam.

Stephanie peered over her shoulder. "I can't even see where it ripped."

"Nope. It's not perfect, but you won't be able to see the fix unless you turn the dress inside out."

Stephanie slipped off the coat and donned the dress. She twisted, trying to see the mended seam. "I can't believe you did it. Thank you."

She stopped at the sound of someone trying to open the locked door.

"Stephanie, are you in there?" It was the director.

Tilly swept her sewing notions back into their box and dropped it all in her bag.

"Yes, Dr. Foster, we're here." She hurried to the door, unlocked it, and threw it open.

Dr. Foster peered in. Her hawkish glare stopped on Tilly.

"I was just showing Miss Bennett where she could keep her things during the performance." Stephanie turned to Tilly with a wild look that screamed *Please back me up.*

"Right," Tilly added quickly. "I don't have much, just my dance bag." She lifted it as if to prove it.

Dr. Foster pursed her lips. Could she smell the deceit? Probably, but she let it drop. Instead she squared her shoulders and clasped her hands in front of herself, looking about as solemn and official as a woman in a cable knit sweater bearing a giant Christmas tree on the front possibly could. "That is the least we can offer, considering. You may leave whatever you like in here. It'll be safe. Did you bring music?"

Tilly fished her phone from the tote and handed it over. "I put together a few tracks. They're in the playlist folder as Playlist One."

Dr. Foster took the phone. "I'm afraid that doesn't mean anything to me, but I'm sure our sound man will know what to do with it." She hesitated. "I don't want to rush you, but the residents and their guests have finished dinner and are on to dessert. Some may be about to retire for the night, if..."

Tilly threw up her hands, understanding immediately. "I'm ready when you are. Just tell me where to go."

CHAPTER TWENTY-TWO

TILLY HAD TO hand it to the Newport Horizons staff. They had worked some impressive holiday magic on the common room. It wasn't just the candlelight or the way it glinted off the wine glasses and the silver on the linen-covered tables. And it wasn't the way the bouquets added a touch of elegance—though they did give her a twinge of pride. It wasn't even the way the massive Christmas tree stood tall and regal beside the stage, twinkling with hundreds of tiny red and green lights.

It was the way all of it came to together, filling the place with a festive spirit she saw reflected on the faces of everyone there, residents and guests alike. She took in each smile and each friendly gaze. But there was one missing.

"Are you looking for Mrs. Rizzetti?"

Tilly pulled back from the crack she'd made in the doorway. "Have you seen her?"

Stephanie nudged Tilly aside and looked through the crack herself. "She was at the table by the stage with her son when I left, but I don't see her now. I hope nothing happened."

A tendril of fear curled in her gut. "Why? What could happen?"

"What you saw in her apartment? That was one of her milder episodes. They're usually worse, especially at night."

Tilly nodded and slid the *zills* on her thumbs and middle fingers. Sundowner's syndrome. That's what Dr. Foster had called it that afternoon.

"I can call her room, if you want."

"No, don't bother her." Or Marco. She forced a smile and tried to pretend everything was fine.

Stephanie must have known it was false because she put her hand lightly on Tilly's arm. "We're all so happy you're here. Everyone was disappointed when the carolers canceled. You're just the sweetest thing for giving up your own Christmas Eve plans to do this."

"I wouldn't want to be anywhere else."

Stephanie patted her shoulder, but their attention was drawn to Dr. Foster walking onstage. She took the microphone and tapped it to quiet the room.

Stephanie winked. "Looks like you're up."

It had been a long time since Tilly experienced butterflies before a performance, but she had them now. Even her butterflies had butterflies. She tried to listen to what Dr. Foster was saying, but the words blurred. She tried to force herself to focus.

"Our carolers, as you know, couldn't make it," the director was saying, "and we're very sorry about that, but I'm excited to announce that we have a last-minute addition to the program. It's something a little out of the ordinary for us, but I'm sure you are going to be as charmed by our surprise entertainer as I am. Straight from her appearance with the world-renowned Belly Dance Divas at the Orange County Arts Palladium, please welcome Tilly Burnett!"

The woman nodded to a man standing beside a tower of sound equipment. He pressed a lever and the audience all waited for the music to begin. And they waited…

Tilly looked out at the crowd of strangers and sighed. This wasn't how this moment was supposed to go. When she'd imagined it, she was dancing for Marco again. Reviving the magical moments from the night before. It hadn't occurred to her that he wouldn't be here.

She leaned against the wall and waited as the sound tech frantically popped cords in and out of their ports, trying to coax sound from his machine.

Stephanie watched, too. "I don't know why this is taking so long. Should I go see what's wrong?"

Tilly shook her head. What difference did it make? She already knew this was a giant mistake. But she couldn't say that. Instead, she fidgeted with her finger cymbals, shook off the nerves and the regret, and gave Stephanie a there's-nothing-to-worry-about smile. Stephanie looked relieved, but Tilly didn't feel any better.

She shouldn't have called Dr. Foster. She shouldn't have come. But it was done, and she had to see it through. As soon as it was over, she'd leave. Get back to her hotel room. Get back to her life.

The seconds stretched into an eternity.

She eyed the sound technician again. But he wasn't looking at the machine anymore. He was searching the room. For what?

Then a figure moved from the shadows near the door and darted across the floor. A man in a black suit was rushing to the sound guy's rescue. Even in the dim light, Tilly recognized that figure, that dark scruff along his jaw, the flip of black hair that brushed his forehead.

Marco.

CHAPTER TWENTY-THREE

ALL EYES IN the banquet hall were on the sound guy and Marco. Was it her imagination or was he wearing a tuxedo? Damn, he looked good. Sharp. Sophisticated. Even better than she remembered, if that were possible. Silently she begged him to look her direction. If she could just see his expression, she'd know. Was he happy to see her? Was he angry? The questions pounded in her chest.

Dr. Foster walked up to the men and blocked her view.

Tilly shook out her arms and tried to breathe. She watched the crowd, waiting for the random clicks and hums from the speakers to settle into music.

She tried to ignore Marco. She couldn't think about him.

Or those eyes.

Or those lips.

Or those hands that had driven her wild for hours.

But if she could just see his face, maybe she'd know. Was it already too late?

The seconds ticked by, and what was left of her confidence slipped into fear.

Her heart pounded. Her lips parched. Maybe there was still time to run.

No. She'd come this far.

She swallowed. Hard. Why was he making her so crazy? Why did she even care about this guy?

But she knew the answer. Marco wasn't just a guy. He was *the* guy. The only one who mattered.

She'd known it last night, she knew it now, and it stripped her bare.

Music filled the speakers, and the crowd came alive.

But it wasn't her music. It was something else.

Just as quickly, the room fell silent again.

Marco and the sound man exchanged congratulatory high-fives. They whispered with Dr. Foster. She nodded and broke away, scanned the room, and when she spotted Tilly at the door, she made her way through the crowd toward her.

"I'm sorry about this." The director's fingers worried themselves into a knot. "I'm afraid our system is incapable of reading the songs from your device. Do you have the music on a disc?"

She did until last night. Her small CD collection had been in her car along with everything else. "All I have is is on my phone."

"I was afraid of that."

Tilly braced for what was coming next. Rejection. Surely a polite one, but still embarrassing.

Dr. Foster shot a quick look back at Marco. At least it didn't appear to be easy for her.

Tilly touched the woman's clasped hands. "It's all right. It's not your fault."

"There is another option," the woman said. "We have several holiday songs available, and Mrs. Rizzetti's son seems to think you might—"

He was watching her now.

Finally, she could see his face. Those wide and wondering eyes, the slight tilt of his head. She found no answers there, only more questions.

But it was enough.

"Holiday music is fine." She blurted it before fear made her mind go blank.

Dr. Foster's hands stopped moving. "Are you sure? Please don't feel obligated. If you—"

"Really. I don't mind."

It wasn't the music she would choose, but the alternative was worse. There were so many eager faces turned her way. There was Marco.

"Whatever you have will be fine. Honestly." She was doing her best to put the anxious woman at ease.

Dr. Foster returned to the sound system and conferred with Marco and the sound tech. Before she knew it, the beginnings of a tune poured out of the speaker. A familiar one that nearly broke her heart.

Jingle Bells.

The crowd clapped, applauding the music and urging her on.

There was no backing out now. She closed her eyes and pushed away the memory of Marco watching her last night, and that dance that had ended with them in his room. She concentrated on her feet and her arms and her hips. On her way to the stage, something new replaced the *baladi* rhythm that usually guided her *zills*. She followed the new rhythm and let it carry her through her dance repertoire. Through moves that were as much a part of her as her breath and her heart beat.

She tried to forget the gorgeous man striding across the room, away from her, his eyes again avoiding hers. He stopped beside a woman she hadn't noticed before. A woman in a striking crimson dress who bopped and swayed to the rhythm and pointed vigorously at Tilly. It was Mrs. Rizzetti, looking as sharp and sophisticated as her son.

Tilly's skin burned at the thought of what Mrs. Rizzetti must be whispering in her son's ear.

But the woman's enthusiasm gave her courage. Quickly, before she could second guess herself, she navigated away from the stage and danced toward Mrs. Rizzetti. The crowd cheered, and it made her bolder. She wasn't going to wait for him to make a move. She'd make one herself.

If she couldn't tell him how sorry she was, she would show him. She sashayed closer, step by step. She tried to keep her eyes on Mrs. Rizzetti, but they gravitated to Marco anyway. Each time, his face was blank, inscrutable. No smile. No twinkle. Not a single sign of forgiveness.

She smiled hard enough for both of them. *Don't be mad. Please don't be mad.*

Finally, a twitch broke his stony expression.

It gave her hope.

Mrs. Rizzetti couldn't look more delighted. She clapped her hands to the music and muttered something to Marco in Italian.

"*Si, mamma.*" The words wrestled out of him as though he were torn between sharing his mother's joy and keeping a grip on his anger.

Tilly focused on Mrs. Rizzetti. She took the woman's hands and nudged her chin toward the dance floor.

The woman's smile widened. Marco's frown deepened, but he didn't try to stop her. Instead, he leaned into his mother's ear and whispered.

The older woman batted him away and muttered something Tilly couldn't understand.

Tilly's resolve weakened. She would have whispered an apology or said something, anything, but Marco glared off in the opposite direction.

He wanted nothing to do with her. That was clear.

She fought the urge to give up. There'd be time to feel sorry for herself later. Right now, she had a show to do, these people deserved that. Mrs. Rizzetti deserved that.

And by the smile radiating off this tiny, surprisingly nimble lady, she'd better get on with it.

Tilly led the woman to the center of the dance floor to a new round of applause. She turned to Mrs. Rizzetti, took both her hands, and shimmied her shoulders until the woman copied the movement.

When she'd mastered that move, Tilly switched to her hips, circling them as though she were drawing slow and wide figure eights on the floor.

Mrs. Rizzetti stumbled through the change. To help, Tilly turned around, so her back faced Mrs. Rizzetti, and continued the movement. Instantly, Mrs. Rizzetti was swaying through the eights with ease.

When *Jingle Bells* finished, another Christmas tune followed, and Mrs. Rizzetti didn't lose a beat. And she wasn't the only one. Tilly scanned the crowd and saw a few other women had stood and were trying the movements themselves. She waved them closer. One by one, the dance floor filled with women eager to dance.

They fanned out around her.

"Ready for something different?" she said to the group over the music. "Follow me."

She moved through a hip drop and hand *floreo* combination at half speed and repeated it.

When a new song began and most of the women had mastered the move, she quickened the pace and combined it with a chest circle and a shoulder shimmy.

Behind her, the women followed along. Hesitantly at first, but with more confidence and vigor after every repetition.

One song became two songs, then three. A few women, obviously winded but grinning wildly, retreated back to their tables, but most stayed on the dance floor.

When the music ran out, only Mrs. Rizzetti and four others remained. Tilly gave them each a hug, and they squeezed her back, giggling like schoolgirls.

"Meravigliosa," Mrs. Rizzetti declared again and again. When the cheering from the crowd died down, Mrs. Rizzetti tugged her off the dance floor. She leaned in close so she could whisper. "You must meet my son."

Tilly tensed. She'd nearly forgotten. She searched the doorway. He was gone.

Mrs. Rizzetti bent closer and whispered, "Don't be shy. He is a nice boy."

"I have no doubt, but…" But what? What could she say?

She relented. The woman tugged her by the elbow. They walked and she scanned the room. He was sitting not far from the door, at a table, alone.

Their gazes met and those dark, mysterious eyes jolted her but his expression offered no clue about his thoughts. If only she could see that wide, rosy smile of his. Hear him call her bella just one more time.

If only she could turn back time...

Mrs. Rizzetti checked that no one was within earshot and bent down to her son, still holding Tilly's hand in hers.

"This is Tilly, the woman I told you about."

He stood, buttoned his tuxedo jacket, and narrowed his eyes. "Hello, Tilly. It's a pleasure to see you again."

CHAPTER TWENTY-FOUR

MARCO'S WORDS WEREN'T angry or hateful. They weren't spiteful. They were ... nothing, and they paralyzed Tilly. She was prepared for anger, but not for this. She straightened and fought the fresh urge to flee.

Maria Rizzetti watched them both. Her head cocked to the side, not understanding. "You know each other?"

"We met yesterday." Marco stared across the room. "Briefly. I would not say we know each other."

The words burned through Tilly.

Mrs. Rizzetti's scowl deepened. She rattled off something in Italian, then tapped at her temples. The tapping grew more rapid and intense. Her face crumpled into a grimace. Then it was gone. She looked up with wide, bewildered eyes. She tapped her temple again.

Marco's apathy vanished. He draped his arm across his mother's shoulders and pulled her close. "It's all right. Let's go back to your room."

Maria Rizzetti looked around the banquet hall and cowered into his embrace. "*Si, papa. Si. Dove siamo?*"

Marco tightened his hold on his mother. He met Tilly's gaze. "I'm sorry. We need to leave."

"Of course." The words scraped out of her, but everything else she wanted to say remained inside. Stuck on her pride and her fear.

He whispered something soothing to his mother. She caught the last of it. "Come with me, bella."

"*Bella, bella, bella,*" the old woman sang to herself. To Tilly she waved, girlishly. "*Buona sera, signorina.*"

Tilly waved and her heart broke.

Marco guided his mother to the doorway.

Tilly wiped away a tear. For herself? For Marco? For the vibrant woman she'd met that day?

"It's a vicious disease."

Dr. Foster's voice startled Tilly from her stupor. The director was standing at her shoulder, staring into the dark corridor where Marco had led his mother.

Tilly blinked away another tear.

The director took her arm and turned her away from the doorway, toward the dance floor where a few couples were grooving to the disco music that had replaced the holiday carols. "Nights tend to be the worst, but it's always unpredictable. Marco tries to be with her during the day when she's at her best. Mornings mostly. But of course he would never let her spend Christmas Eve alone."

"No, I'm sure he wouldn't."

"I want to thank you again for tonight. I really can't tell you how much it means to everyone. That dance lesson was a joy to watch."

Tilly watched couples doing the hustle, or trying to, and there was one group of women who had taken over a corner of the dance floor to practice their belly dance moves. It lightened her heart to see their joy, but it didn't change anything. She didn't belong here.

"If you'd ever like to come back," Dr. Foster said, "we'd be delighted to have you. I haven't seen our residents this lively in quite some time."

"Thank you. It's been wonderful, but I should be going."

She reached for the director's hand and shook it. "Thank you for everything. I'll just get my things and see myself out."

"Are you sure? You're welcome to stay."

"No, I really should be going."

"Of course." The older woman patted her hand and for the first time looked almost maternal. "It's Christmas."

Christmas in a hotel room. A sanctuary where she could be alone and not pretend it didn't hurt.

The light was on in the director's office and Stephanie had hung her coat on the back of the desk chair. Tilly wrapped herself in it. This was it.

It wasn't the way she'd imagined the night would end. Maybe that was her fault. Scratch that. It was definitely her fault. She was the one who jumped to conclusions. She was the one who sneaked out when he was sleeping. He was better off without her. He probably already knew that.

She dropped her tote on the desk and plunged her hand in and fished around for her keys. She found the edge of her makeup case, her sewing case, her extra hairpins. She dug deeper.

She couldn't shake the feeling that she still hadn't apologized. There was no doubt Marco was glad to be rid of her, but he still deserved that much, didn't he? He deserved to know she'd undo it all if she could, even if it wouldn't change anything.

She knew the way to Mrs. Rizzetti's apartment. She could go up and knock on the door.

No way. He needed to focus on his mother.

Her eyes landed on Dr. Foster's notepad with the perfectly sharpened pencil beside it.

Ten minutes later, she was back in the banquet hall. There was no sign of Marco, no sign of his mother. But Dr. Foster was standing beside one of the outer tables, chatting with a couple. Tilly pinched the folded paper between her fingers. She'd wait until the director was finished, and then she'd approach her.

She waited. The conversation went on.

"Excuse me."

The voice surprised her, but when she turned and found the tiny woman beside her she recognized her immediately. It was the women who had first joined her and Mrs. Rizzetti on the dance floor, and, as far as Tilly could tell, she'd never left it.

"I don't want to bother you, but I was just wondering, well, a few of us were wondering, actually, if you might show us again how to do that thing you were doing with your arms." The woman extended her arms to her sides and waved them like cooked spaghetti noodles.

"Snake arms. You've nearly got it, just slow the movement down, and the arms should move in opposition."

"In opposition?" The woman's forehead wrinkled. "Could you, perhaps, demonstrate?"

Tilly glanced at the small group of women on the dance floor, standing and gaping in her direction. She looked at her letter. She looked at Dr. Foster, who was still deep in conversation. "Of course. I'd be happy to."

She set down the paper and her things at an empty table and took the woman's outreached hand. Together they walked back to the dance floor.

CHAPTER TWENTY-FIVE

MARCO SAT IN the cold darkness of his mother's balcony, grazing from a platter of her gingerbread cookies, watching the lights along the waterfront below, and trying to forget about Tilly.

It wasn't working.

The soft padding of his mother's slippers across the floor told him she had emerged from her room. He rose from the white wicker chair. "How are you, *mamma*? Can I get you anything?"

She stepped out onto the small landing and tightened the belt of her velvety robe. "I'm fine. Don't worry. The boats are so lovely, aren't they? So many lights, like so many Christmas trees." She touched his arm, her thin, blue-veined fingers curling around his wrist. She shivered.

"You shouldn't be out here. Let's go in." He took her hand and ushered her back inside, into the warm and safe cocoon of her apartment.

"The cookies. Don't forget them."

"Don't worry. You know they're my favorite." He swept up the platter with his free hand and put them down on the coffee table inside. He deposited his mother in the recliner in front of her television.

"I know, *cucchiolo*. Since you were a boy. You never change."

She pulled a folded wool blanket off the chair's arm and onto her lap. She tucked it around herself, like she was defending herself against an arctic freeze, not the mild temperatures that constituted winter in Southern California. She grabbed the remote, clicked on the television, and skipped channels until she landed on something black and white. One of the old Hollywood classics.

"Neither do you, *mamma*." He patted her shoulder and wandered back to the window. Even in the darkness, it was like he could see to the end of the world. So wide open, so empty. So altogether different from the frenetic Piazza del Duomo outside his family's apartment. Especially this time of year when there would be so much activity. Here, there were no dustings of snow. No family gatherings. No Christmas Eve Mass. Not much of anything that resembled the holidays of his youth.

"Are you happy, Marco?"

His mother's question startled him. "Of course. I'm with you."

She clucked and rearranged her blanket. "You are a good boy."

"Sometimes."

She wagged her finger at him. "You are a good boy, but you are stupid."

"Excuse me?"

"I saw how you looked at her."

"Who?"

"You know. The dancer."

He stared hard at the glass. At the bay and the golden reflections of a thousand tiny lights, but mostly at the darkness that embraced them. He didn't trust himself to speak.

"There is something between you two, *no*?"

"No." He shook his head, punctuating the truth of it, for his own sake if not hers.

"Come here."

He felt like a child again, following her commands. When he approached, she reached out and took his hand in both of her own.

He stared at her fingers, taking in every wrinkle and vein. Those hands had been so strong once. They had carried him before he could walk. Lifted him when he fell. They cooked and cleaned and cared for him. Now they trembled with age. Feeble, fragile. But still they consoled him.

"I could not ask for a better son. You have made me happy when I thought I had used up all my happiness."

"Don't talk like that."

"I will. I must, because you don't see what you are doing to yourself. You have given me too much, Marco. It's not your fault. It's mine because I let you. I wanted to have you all to myself for the time I have left."

"*Mamma*, stop." Her words ripped into him, shredding his resolve.

"I won't. I have had a wonderful life, *cucchiolo*. I had a wonderful husband, wonderful sons, especially you, still my *bambino*. And now I get to be here, in this beautiful place with the ocean breezes and the palm trees and the wicked sea gulls that foul my table."

He laughed.

"Yes!" Her eyes glinted with life. So much life. "For you, I want more laughter. More love."

"I have that." He squeezed her hand gently. "I have all I need."

She shook her head. "No, my boy. Not yet."

He thought of Tilly. Seeing her again had made everything so much more difficult. He'd told himself a hundred times it didn't matter that she'd left. That she'd done them both a favor by doing it. He didn't believe it at first. He'd wanted her to stay until she had to leave. Until her tour resumed. But that gave them, what? Two days? It wouldn't be enough. And that was the bottom line, wasn't it? Those fleeting moments together would never be enough.

If only he could have said goodbye. That was his only regret now.

"Those cookies." She nudged her chin at the platter. "Do you plan to eat them all alone?"

"Don't you want any?"

"You know I can't have sweets. Doctor's orders. They are for you, but perhaps you want to share? I know someone who fancies gingerbread."

He recognized that twinkle in his mother's eye. It was a plan.

Ten minutes later, he entered the banquet room with the platter of cookies as his cover. He walked them to the dessert table and set them down beside the picked-over plates of single-portion cakes and pastries. A few of the more alert guests gravitated to the fresh offering like bees to honey.

Then he saw her. Blond curls and red lace at the center of the dance floor. She was coaching a group through belly dance moves, adapting the motions to the disco rhythms playing on the stereo. He smiled despite himself.

He wasn't too late.

Relief mingled with hope, but what did it really mean? Maybe nothing. Maybe everything.

Adrenaline shot through him as he watched her, and he paced the room's perimeter, debating what to say, when he noticed her red purse sitting beside a bulging tote on an empty table. His heart leaped. He wouldn't have to do anything. He wouldn't have to *say* anything. He could simply wait. Eventually she would return to the table for her things. She would come to him.

He slid into the chair beside her things, and that's when he saw it. A folded sheet of paper with his name written on it.

He pulled it closer. There was no mistaking. His name was written there in pencil: Marco Rizzetti.

He could see more was written inside. Was it an explanation? It was so tempting to open it, but he couldn't. It was wrong.

He pushed it back, but it was already too late.

She was walking toward him.

CHAPTER TWENTY-SIX

MARCO WATCHED THE woman he'd prayed to see and whom he feared to see. He watched her glide across the floor, the beads of her scarlet costume sparkling brighter than the table-side candles as her hips and shoulders swayed. He stared at that incredible, confident figure, searching for the funny and kind and amazing woman he'd held in his arms the night before.

"You came back." Tilly's words pinned him with their intensity. Her blue eyes smoldered. "I didn't think you would."

He stood and his chest tightened. His pulse raced. He could have downed an entire pitcher of water if there'd been one in sight.

She glanced at the door and ran her tongue across her top lip. Maybe she was thirsty too. Or maybe she just knew how unbelievably sexy that looked and enjoyed torturing him.

"Is your mother all right?"

He sighed. He wasn't the only one with a reason to be angry.

"I should have told you the truth."

"Why didn't you?" It was a question, but it was also an accusation and it caught him by surprise.

"I didn't know how." He raked guilty fingers through his hair. "You assumed she was gone, and I didn't know how to explain it without making everything complicated."

"Right. Because this isn't complicated?" She rubbed her forehead and chuckled softly. "It doesn't matter. You could have just told me it was none of my business."

"It wasn't that."

She nodded, but she didn't believe him. He could see it in the thin line of her lips, the dull cast of her eyes. She touched the folded paper beside her purse.

"What is that?" He tried not to sound interested, but he knew he'd failed.

She brushed her fingertips over his name.

"I wrote you a letter. An apology, actually. I wanted you to know I was sorry about this morning. About leaving without an explanation."

That terrible feeling returned. That pang of loss and regret that had seared through him when he realized she was gone. The ache he'd been fighting all day.

Pride made him shrug and look away.

"Actually, it was pretty stupid."

"How so?" He braced himself for a fresh wave of pain.

She stared at the paper and outlined tiny figure eights on it with her red lacquered fingernail. "I was jealous."

He'd imagined dozens of excuses, but not this one. "Jealous of what?"

Her glance shot up but just as quickly skittered away. "I saw your mother's text by accident." She winced. "Maybe not entirely by accident, but that's not the point. I saw it, and I thought if was from your girlfriend."

"I don't have a girlfriend." He had told her that. He was sure of it.

She stared at the ground. "I know. You did." Her voice was so small.

"You didn't believe me?" The accusation hurt, but more so because it was justified. He shook his head. "I guess I deserve it. I wasn't honest with you. Not about my mother. But I don't have a girlfriend. That is the truth."

"I know. I was wrong. I shouldn't have jumped to conclusions. I just thought maybe it was part of the deal. The flirting at the bar, all the attention you get from women, and then you have a bedroom right above the restaurant? I figured you were the kind of guy who plays around, and I thought I was all right with that..." Her voice faltered. She stopped.

He touched her shoulder. "It's not like that. I'm not like that. Maybe I flirt. That's all. I have never brought someone up to my room. Ask anyone. Ask Abby."

Her eyes glistened, and she cocked her head to the side. "Then why me?"

It was a good question, and it was the one he'd been asking himself all day. "I don't know." He chuckled, but stopped. "That isn't true. I like you. A lot. And I thought it would be all right. Safe. Abby told me you would be leaving. I thought we could have something for just a night or two and that would be it. But when I woke up and you were gone, all I could think about was getting you back."

A wispy curl fell over her cheek. He reached out and guided it back behind her ear. She nuzzled into his touch, and it nearly undid him. The feel of her, the warmth of her. Everything he'd felt last night. Everything he wanted to feel again.

But he couldn't give in. As much as he wanted her, nothing had changed. He shoved his hand back into his pocket. He only came to say goodbye.

"What you did," he said, "it was for the best."

Tears welled in her eyes, and her lower lip quivered.

He looked away. He didn't want to hurt her. It was just the facts.

"You're still leaving," he said. "You won't—"

He couldn't say it. The weight of it nearly crushed his chest.

"No."

The word ripped through him. It shredded him. Why was she making this more difficult? He should have stayed upstairs. He could have lived without goodbye, but how was he going to live with this?

"Yes." He choked out the word. "You're leaving."

"No. No!"

Was she crying or laughing? She grabbed his shirt in her fists and pulled herself up till they were nose to nose, lips to lips. He stared at the silvery flecks in her blue eyes and breathed in the vanilla scent of her hair. Her bloodshot eyes held him, and she said, "I'm not going anywhere."

He heard the words but they didn't register. Her lips were too close, her everything was too close.

She loosened her grip and dropped back on her heels. "I said, I'm not leaving."

Was it a joke? Was she playing with him? He stepped back, trying to make sense of it. "But the tour?"

Her cheeks glistened with a stream of tears. She shook her head.

She wasn't making sense. None of this was making sense.

"Your tour's off?"

She shook her head again. She was sniffling and dabbing at her nose, but she was smiling too. A hesitant smile that was growing wider by the second.

His hopes surged.

She grabbed his hands.

"Tonight's performance was my last as a Belly Dance Diva. I quit."

Her words sliced through the air, cleaving everything he believed. Unhinging his white-knuckle grip on his world.

"You did? How? Why?" The words sputtered out before he could consider them, before he could stop them.

"I don't want to be on the tour. I don't want that life."

She weaved her fingers between his and squeezed them. He could feel her unease, her fear.

He squeezed her back then pulled out of her grip. He wanted to step away, but he couldn't. It was something in her eyes, still wet and glistening with emotion. So unsure. He raised his fingers to her cheeks, touched that soft porcelain skin, ran his thumb over her tender pink lips. He couldn't walk away from her. Not now. Not ever. But none of this made sense.

"You told me you loved it. The freedom, the independence. A modern nomad, a traveling gypsy."

"I know." Her gaze dropped away. "I used to, I think. I wanted to. I don't know. I guess I thought I was supposed to. Maybe I just didn't have anything else."

Her smile vanished. Her sparkle was losing its shine.

He squeezed her fingers, trying to bring it back.

"You have me."

Her eyes shot up to him.

"Do I?"

Hope flamed in her expression and burned his heart wide open.

"You do." In that moment, he knew he loved her. He'd loved her when he found her frightened and alone in the parking lot, and when she'd teased him from the stage. He'd loved her at the first smirk of her ruby red lips and that first brush of her fingers against his on the martini glass. He wanted to tell her, to shout it to anyone who would listen, but instead he folded her in his arms.

He pulled her close and she pressed herself against him, as eager for him as he was for her.

"Are you sure?" She bit her lip.

"Yes, bella. A million times yes."

Their lips collided and it was like no other kiss before it. No hesitation. No holding back. It was complete surrender to the moment and to whatever future lie ahead.

It was everything, and he could have kissed her forever if the sound of someone nearby clearing her throat hadn't forced him to come up for air.

The director was standing beside them with a wild, what-on-earth-are-you-doing look and doing her best to block the view from the other party guests.

Tilly jerked away, guilt carved into her face. "Dr. Foster, hi, we were just, uh..."

"I see that." Dr. Foster shot glances behind her like a B-movie lookout man. "But maybe you could take this somewhere else?"

Tilly pulled away. "I'm so sorry. We didn't mean to—"

He pulled her close again and draped his arm around her shoulders. "Of course we did."

Tilly giggled and molded against him. "Okay, maybe we did, but—"

He leaned forward. "But we were just leaving."

"I don't mean to sound old-fashioned, but, you know, maybe that would be for the best." Dr. Foster walked back to her table, but she kept her eyes on them.

He lifted one of Tilly's hands to his lips and kissed her fingertips. "We could go to my place. The restaurant is closed."

"No, I don't think so."

"No?" He dropped her hand. Hurt. Confused.

She reached over the table and pulled a royal blue plastic card from her purse. She raised it so he could see the golden Newport Bay Club and Resort logo, and she wiggled it. A wicked, sexy smile crept across her face. "I have a better idea."

He grabbed her around the waist and caught her lips with his. After a long kiss, he pulled away and gazed at her, seeing all his love reflected back in those sweet, blue eyes. "Whatever you have in mind," he whispered, "I'm in."

CHAPTER TWENTY-SEVEN

THE TABLETOP RUMBLED to the *thump-thump-thumping* beat of the electronic music pumping through the sound system of the Sultan's Tent bar, and the air teemed with hoots and clicks from the noise makers handed out with New Year's Eve hats and tiaras at the door. Tilly was so caught up in the distractions she didn't notice the cell phones buzzing at her elbow.

Abby did.

"Look at that." Abby tapped her screen. "It's midnight in New York."

Tilly swiped her own screen and read the Happy New Year message Melanie had sent with a string of party emojis.

"The show must be over." Abby typed in a reply, then switched off her phone. "What do you think they're doing?"

Tilly hit the send button on her own reply. "No idea, but I'm sure it's big. Garrett wouldn't waste an opportunity to throw a party."

"Do you miss it?"

"What?"

"Being a Belly Dance Diva."

That reality still hadn't sunk in. The past week had been such a blur. So much had happened, so much had changed. She was still trying to process most of it.

"Technically, I'm still in the group. As head costume designer, I'll just be making costumes instead of dancing. And I won't have to travel. I've been busy, though. I've sketched some ideas for the summer lineup that I want to run by Garrett when he gets back to town. As soon as I find space to work, I'll start mocking up samples."

"How much space do you need?"

"I don't know. Enough for a sewing machine and a few racks. To start with anyway."

"You're welcome to use the studio's storage room. You can consider it a perk of your other new job. Wait, I almost forgot." She yanked her purse off the back of her chair and pulled out a ball of black fabric. She tossed it to Tilly.

Tilly unrolled the black spaghetti-strap tank with the hot-pink Shimmy Shop logo emblazoned on the front. "Look at that. I was hoping Santa would leave one of these in my stocking."

"I'm just glad Santa brought me someone to cover Melanie's classes while she's on tour. It looks like we both scored." She laughed and cast a sidelong glance toward Marco, who was filling drinks behind the bar. "And speaking of scored, how's that going?"

Marco winked at Tilly and a warm feeling spread through her. She shifted and played with the speared olive in her martini glass. "Pretty well, actually."

"Just pretty well?"

"I don't know. I haven't done this in a while."

"Done what? Had a guy around for more than a few days?"

"Something like that." She shredded the edges of her napkin and sucked in her lips to hide a giddy grin when Marco approached with a tray of champagne flutes and a bottle.

"What did I tell you?" Abby took a glass. "Marco always takes care of us. Best bartender ever."

"For a few more days anyway," he said. "But don't worry. I'll train my replacement well."

"Replacement? What?" Abby looked at Tilly. "Did you know about this?"

She nodded.

"Why didn't you tell me? Where are you going?"

"Nowhere. But starting Monday, I'm the new assistant manager."

Abby squealed. "Really? That's fantastic. I'm so happy for you. We definitely have to toast to that."

Janaya leaned over from the adjacent table, where she was sitting with the rest of the Shimmy Shop group. One of her dreadlocks fell over her shoulder. "Are those for all of us?"

"Of course, my friend." He handed her one.

"What happened to bella?" She pretended to pout.

Tilly stiffened. Marco must have sensed it because he draped his arm around her shoulder and kissed the side of her head. "I have only one bella now. At least as long as she'll have me."

She glanced up, and they locked gazes. It didn't matter how often she looked into his Hershey's kiss eyes, it sent sweet tingles through her every time.

He dropped his chin. "Did you tell them?"

Abby jerked her champagne away from her lips. "Tell us what?"

Abby's boyfriend, Derek, slid through the crowd and retook his seat beside her. "Excellent! Somebody ordered champagne. I was just thinking we need—"

A half-dozen female heads turned his direction. "Sh!"

He hunched his shoulders to his ears and took the last glass from the tray. "Sorry! What did I say?"

Abby leaned over. "Marco and Tilly were about to tell us some big news."

Tilly's cheeks ignited. "It isn't *big* news."

Marco looked at Tilly. "It isn't small news."

"Just tell us!"

Tilly tapped Marco's leg. "You do it."

"No, bella, you do it."

Abby slammed her hand on the table. "For crying out loud, somebody tell us so we can drink."

"Okay." Tilly giggled. "We're moving in together."

"What?" Abby squealed. "When? Why doesn't anybody tell me anything?"

"It just happened. We signed the rental papers today. I wanted to tell you, but we decided to do it together. Don't be mad."

"I'm not mad." Abby grabbed Tilly's hand and squeezed. "As long as you're happy, I'm happy." She jabbed Marco in the arm. "For both of you."

Tilly smiled at Marco, and that feeling was there again. Like nobody else existed. Just him and her, and a whole lifetime ahead of them.

Abby raised her glass. "We need a toast. Toast, toast, toast."

The others lifted their glasses and took up the chant.

Marco held up his hand and they quieted. "This is one my father taught me." He lifted his glass. "Here's to a bright New Year, and a fond farewell to the old. Here's to the things that are yet to come, and to the memories that we hold.'"

He squeezed Tilly's hand, and everyone around the table cheered and clinked and drank again.

Tilly stood beside him. "I'd like to add just one more thing: a new year is a wonderful new beginning, and my wish for all of you is that this year will be your very best yet." She lifted Marco's fingers to her lips and kissed them. "I know mine will be."

His eyes shimmered when he leaned down and kissed her, a long, tender kiss that made her toes dance and her heart soar. In a whisper only she could hear, he added. "Mine, too, bella."

On the table, Tilly's phone vibrated on the table.

Abby grabbed it. "Terrible timing! I'll tell them to call back later."

Tilly didn't take her eyes off of Marco. "Sure. Or send it to voice mail."

Abby tapped the screen and put the phone to her ear. "Tilly Bennett's Party Line. How can we help you?" Her goofy grin vanished. Her shoulders pulled back. "Yes, sir. She is here. Of course. I'll get her." She muted the phone and held it out to Tilly. "It's the cops."

Tilly took the phone and made her way out of the bar. She found a quiet spot on a bench, away from the door.

"This is Tilly Bennett."

"Miss Bennett? This is Officer Grant."

Ten minutes later, Marco walked out with her Spanish shawl and found her sitting on a bench, her phone cradled in her lap.

"Are you all right? I thought you might be cold." He handed her the shawl, hesitantly.

She wrapped the soft fabric around her shoulders. "They found my car."

"That's great. Isn't it great?" He frowned. "Is it all right?"

"Yeah. I think so. It sounds like everything's still there. The officer said there wasn't any damage, just some trash, food wrappers, and sand. They picked up a couple kids who told them they borrowed it to go down to Baja."

"Borrowed?"

"Yeah. But the security footage from your restaurant showed the break-in. You didn't tell me you gave them security footage."

"I didn't know if it would make a difference."

She took his hand. "It did. They were able to ID one of the kids because she was in the system. When they tracked her down, she told them where to find the car."

"She?"

Tilly sighed and gave him a you-never-can-tell-about-people shrug.

"So, you're good, right? You're going to get all your stuff back."

She stared at her lap again. Not seeing anything, but seeing everything. Maybe for the first time. She squeezed his hand and wove her fingers between his. "I am good, but it has nothing to do with all that stuff. I haven't even missed it. Not really. I don't need any of it. I never lost what was important."

He raised his hand to her cheek and brushed it. "Funny, that sounds familiar."

"Funny, I knew you'd say that. But you were right." She squeezed his hand. "You won't hold it against me, will you?"

"Of course I will. I'm going to hold it against you for a very long time. Starting now." He leaned in and gave her a slow, we've-got-all-the-time-in-the-world kiss.

THE END

***

Have you read all the books in the *California Belly Dance Romance* series?

Shimmy for Me (Book 1)
Dance with Me (Book 2)
Another Dance (Book 3)
Jingly Bells (Book 4)

Visit www.DeAnnaCameron.com for details

AUTHOR'S NOTE

I appreciate you taking the time to read *Jingly Bells.* If you enjoyed it, please consider leaving a review at your favorite e-retailer or Goodreads.com. Your support makes a real difference and would be truly appreciated.

If you'd like to know more about me, please visit my website at www.DeAnnaCameron.com.

GLOSSARY

ASSUIT: A textile of cotton or linen mesh featuring designs crafted from metal strips threaded through the mesh. Its history dates back to ancient Egypt.

BALADI: An Arabic word meaning "my country" often used to refer to traditional music found in rural villages. Also refers to this popular rhythm: *dum-dum-tekka-tek-dum-tekka-tek*.

FLOREO: A Spanish word meaning "flourish," which refers to graceful hand and wrist movements incorporated into many belly dance styles.

TAQSIM: A slow melody usually played without percussive instruments during which a dancer or dancers improvise.

TRIBAL STYLE BELLY DANCE: A primarily improvisational style of dance performed in a group, usually drawing from folkloric influences in the Middle East, North Africa, Spain, and India, as well as modern influences.

ZILLS: Small metallic finger cymbals played by belly dancers and others.

RECIPES

MARCO'S CHRISTMAS WISH COCKTAIL

When I wrote the opening scene of *Jingly Bells*, I was reminded of a cocktail that featured melted vanilla ice cream I had years ago during a press event at the Ritz-Carlton Laguna Niguel. I've re-created it several times at home with different tweaks to the recipe, but this one is my favorite. You can substitute milk, half and half, or heavy cream for the ice cream, but the ice cream gives it an extra richness that really makes this drink special.

Ingredients:
4 parts melted vanilla ice cream (premium variety)
3 parts white cocoa creme de cacao
2 parts peppermint schnapps
1 part vodka
Ice
Crushed candy canes

Prepare the martini glass by rimming it with the crushed candy canes. Fill a cocktail shaker with ice. Pour the melted vanilla ice cream, white cocoa creme de cacao, peppermint schnapps, and vodka over the ice. Cover the shaker and shake. Strain into a martini glass and serve.

MRS. RIZZETTI'S SOFT GINGERBREAD COOKIES

Nothing puts me in the holiday mood like the smell of gingerbread baking in the oven. This is the recipe for the kind of chewy gingerbread I envisioned Mrs. Rizzetti sharing with Marco and Tilly. I hope you love it as much as I do.

Ingredients:
3/4 cup molasses
1/3 cup light brown sugar
1/3 cup water
1/8 cup butter, softened
3 1/4 cups all-purpose flour
1 teaspoon baking soda
2 teaspoon ground ginger
1 teaspoon ground allspice
1 teaspoon ground cinnamon
1/2 teaspoon ground cloves

Mix the molasses, brown sugar, water, and butter in a large bowl until smooth. In a separate bowl, combine the flour, baking soda, allspice, ginger, cloves, and cinnamon. Add the dry ingredients to the wet mixture and stir until well blended. Cover and chill for at least three hours.

Preheat the oven to 350 degrees F (175 degrees C). Lightly flour a surface, then roll out the dough to a 1/4-inch thickness. Cut into desired shapes. Place the cookies an inch apart on ungreased cookie sheets.

Bake for 8 to 10 minutes. Remove the cookies from the cookie sheets and cool on wire racks.

Decorate with Cookie Icing (see Baker's Note) or your favorite icing.

Yield will vary, depending on cookie shapes and sizes.

BAKER'S NOTE: Make Cookie Icing by blending 2 cups confectioners' sugar with 4 tablespoons milk, and 1 teaspoons vanilla or almond extract. Fill a squeeze bottle with the icing, decorate cooled cookies, and allow the icing to dry several hours before handling or storing.

ACKNOWLEDGMENTS

Every story has its challenges and this one was no different. Two people in particular offered invaluable help through some tricky spots: Christina Alexandra, for her emergency-response knowledge, and Denise Muir, for her considerable Italian language skills. I thank them both for their generous assistance.

I would also like to thank the fans of the California Belly Dance Romance series who keep me motivated to write about the spirited lives and loves of the Shimmy Shop women. I'm especially gratefully to this extraordinary group of readers: Abigail, Alice, Christina, Clarissa, Jasmine, Jennifer, Laura, Michelle, Shannon, and Tracy.

Finally, I want to thank my dear friends and family for their continuing support and encouragement. It means the world to me, and I count my lucky stars for each and every one of you.